"She's dead! Jessica is dead!" Jessica Wakefield's identical twin sister, Elizabeth, sobbed wildly into the coarse knit of Luke Shepherd's sweater. Her new boyfriend's arms felt warm and safe around her—but Elizabeth could not be comforted. Behind her, on the bed of Jessica's room at Pembroke Manor, a body lay facedown on blood-soaked sheets—a girl with golden hair, exactly the same shade as Elizabeth's.

The sixteen-year-old twins had traveled to London for a summer internship at the *London Journal*. Not a week had gone by before Jessica's new boyfriend, Robert Pembroke, had invited them to spend a long weekend at his family's country manor. Jessica, of course, had been thrilled about the invitation, but Elizabeth had had misgivings from the start. And now, as Elizabeth stared at the blond-haired body on the bed she wished they had never even left California.

"I knew Jessica was in danger!" Elizabeth cried, pounding her fists against Luke's hard chest. "I should have warned her. I should have warned her."

SWEET VALLEY High®

A DATE WITH A WEREWOLF

**Written by
Kate William**

**Created by
FRANCINE PASCAL**

BANTAM BOOKS
NEW YORK · TORONTO · LONDON · SYDNEY · AUCKLAND

RL 6, age 12 and up

A DATE WITH A WEREWOLF
A Bantam Book / May 1994

Sweet Valley High® is a registered trademark of Francine Pascal
Conceived by Francine Pascal
Produced by Daniel Weiss Associates, Inc.
33 West 17th Street
New York, NY 10011
Cover art by Bruce Emmett

ISBN: 0-553-56228-2

Published simultaneously in the United States and Canada

Bantam Books are published by Bantam Books, a division of Bantam
Doubleday Dell Publishing Group, Inc. Its trademark, consisting of the
words "Bantam Books" and the portrayal of a rooster, is Registered in
U.S. Patent and Trademark Office and in other countries. Marca
Registrada. Bantam Books, 1540 Broadway, New York, New York 10036.

PRINTED IN THE UNITED STATES OF AMERICA

OPM   0 9 8 7 6 5 4 3 2 1

In memory of Kelly Weil

Chapter 1

"She's dead! Jessica is dead!" Jessica Wakefield's identical twin sister, Elizabeth, sobbed wildly into the coarse knit of Luke Shepherd's sweater. Her new boyfriend's arms felt warm and safe around her—as they had the day before, when Luke had kissed her seriously for the first time. But Elizabeth could not be comforted. Behind her, on the bed of Jessica's room at Pembroke Manor, a body lay facedown on blood-soaked sheets—a girl with golden hair, exactly the same shade as Elizabeth's.

The sixteen-year-old twins had traveled to London for a summer internship at the *London Journal*. Not a week had gone by before Jessica's new boyfriend, Robert Pembroke, had invited them to spend a long weekend at his family's country manor. Jessica, of course, had been thrilled about the invitation, but Elizabeth had had misgivings from the start. And now, as Elizabeth stared at the blond-haired body on the bed she wished they had never even left California.

"I knew Jessica was in danger!" Elizabeth cried, pounding her fists against Luke's hard chest. "I should have warned her. I should have warned her."

"Warned me about what?" said a familiar, sleepy voice. Elizabeth whirled, blue-green eyes wide. Jessica was standing in the doorway, yawning. Her hair was disheveled, and her eyes looked tired, and her satiny pink nightgown was wrinkled from sleep, but besides being unaccustomed to getting up at dawn on a Saturday, Jessica seemed like a perfectly healthy teenager.

"You're not dead!" Elizabeth cried, almost knocking her sister over with a bear hug.

"Then who *is*?" asked Luke.

"Dead? Why did you think I was—" Elizabeth felt her sister's body freeze as Jessica saw the bloody girl on the bed. "Oh, my—"

Before Jessica could react further, Andrew Thatcher, London's chief of police and another weekend guest at Pembroke Manor, pushed past the twins into the room. Behind him was Lord Pembroke himself, accompanied by Lady Pembroke, their son Robert, and several servants.

"We heard screams," Robert said, staring wildly at Jessica, his eyes full of concern. "Are you all right?"

The chief of police reached for the dead girl's shoulder and gently turned the body over. Then he cried out and stepped back, shaken. The murdered girl was Joy Singleton, his fiancée.

And her throat had been ripped open . . . *as if by a wild beast*.

2

The words roared into Elizabeth's mind, unbidden. She had first heard them on Monday morning, the twins' first day of work at the *London Journal*. As high-school interns, they would never have been allowed to cover such a grisly murder. But, wanting to be where the excitement was, Jessica and Elizabeth had rushed through their seemingly trivial missing-Yorkie assignment, sneaking off to the Essex Street murder scene.

Elizabeth would never forget the sight of Dr. Cameron Neville's body, lying facedown in a pool of blood that was slowly soaking into the floral-patterned carpet. And Elizabeth would never forget the clear, dispassionate voice of Lucy Friday, the *London Journal* crime desk editor: *"The victim's throat has been ripped open, as if by a wild beast."*

The doctor's murder wasn't the first one in London recently to fit that pattern. Elizabeth, Jessica, and Luke—an intern with the arts and literature section of the newspaper—had been doing some sleuthing into the bizarre incidents. And Luke, at least, was seriously convinced that they were the work of a werewolf.

And as if to add credence to the werewolf theory, some of the Pembrokes' sheep had been found with their throats ripped open—just hours before Joy's murder.

Elizabeth shuddered, remembering the flowering wolfsbane Luke had pointed out to her in a nearby grove Friday afternoon. According to Luke, who was an expert on werewolves, medieval legend said the wolfsbane bloomed only when a werewolf was hunting prey.

3

She reached beneath the collar of her flannel nightgown to finger the silver pendant that hung around her neck. Luke had given it to her. "It will protect you," he had said, clasping the chain around her neck. The pendant showed a five-pointed star—a pentagram—in a circle, with the image of a wolf in its center.

Normally, Elizabeth would have laughed at the notion of needing protection from werewolves. She had always been considered the rational, responsible twin, unlike her more impulsive sister, Jessica. But ideas that would have sounded ridiculous to Elizabeth under the bright California sun somehow seemed more reasonable when voiced through an English fog—especially when voiced by sensitive, handsome Luke. Elizabeth had known Luke for less than a week but she was falling fast for him, despite her feelings for her boyfriend, Todd Wilkins, back in California.

Besides, the evidence from the other victims did point to a murderer who was not quite . . . human.

Now, pleasant, if a little vapid, pretty Joy had been murdered in the same way. Elizabeth felt unsteady and was grateful for Luke's steadying hand on her elbow. Her mind was racing. *Joy had been murdered in Jessica's room,* she thought wildly, *in Jessica's bed.* In the dark, it would have been impossible for the murderer to tell one sleeping blonde from another. *Could Jessica have been the real target?*

Thatcher, visibly trying to collect himself, seemed to be thinking along similar lines. "Jessica," he asked in a strained voice, "Joy's room was across the hall

4

from yours. Why was she sleeping in here instead?"

For once, Elizabeth noted, her sister didn't seem at all concerned about what she looked like. Tears streamed down Jessica's face, and her golden hair was tangled. Jessica had known Joy for only one day, but Elizabeth knew she had liked Thatcher's pretty, young fiancée. And the sight of that bloody bed would scare anyone.

Except for Robert Pembroke, Jr., it seemed. He was as disagreeable as ever, Elizabeth noticed. She scowled as the younger Lord Pembroke turned to two of the servants and began barking out orders.

"Alistair," he said to tall, thin Alistair Crane. "Call the constable right away. Set up extra chairs in the parlor, and be prepared to serve tea." He turned to the pretty, brown-haired cook. "Maria, put the water on, and assemble the other servants."

Then he placed a protective arm around Jessica's trembling shoulders, and Elizabeth pursed her lips at the sight. She couldn't stand Robert's arrogance and his aristocratic airs, and she hated the fact that he and Jessica had become so close. But Jessica gazed gratefully at him through her tears.

"Joy knocked on my door in the middle of the night," Jessica explained haltingly to the chief of police. "She asked me to switch rooms with her. She said she couldn't sleep with the full moon shining in her window."

Beware the full moon. The words came to Elizabeth's mind out of nowhere, and she remembered the scary old lady hissing them at Jessica the day the twins had arrived at their London dormi-

5

tory—HIS, or Housing for International Students. A few days later, a gypsy fortune-teller had given Jessica the same warning. *Beware the full moon.*

Jessica seemed calmer now, but as Elizabeth stared at her twin, she felt a wave of terror. *Jessica is in horrible danger.*

Emily Cartwright picked up Saturday morning's edition of the *London Journal.* "Here's another princess story!" she exclaimed to her friends Lina Smith and Portia Albert. "But that's a frightfully bad little photograph with it. All you can see is a blur of blond hair."

The three girls were huddled around the table in the kitchen of HIS. Breakfast wouldn't be served officially for another hour, but Emily and Lina were up early for a day of sight-seeing, and Portia had an early rehearsal for *A Common Man,* the play in which she was making her London stage debut. The girls were fixing themselves an early breakfast of toast and orange marmalade.

"I suppose it's because I'm Australian," Emily said, gesturing with the newspaper, "but I do not understand this all-consuming passion you Brits have for gossip about the royal family. I was addicted to it when I first got here, but now even *I'm* getting tired of it."

"Sometimes I don't understand it myself," Lina remarked, running her fingers through her short brown hair. "So, Portia, what time is your play rehears—"

"Listen to this morning's bit," Emily interrupted, pointing to a banner headline across the front page of

6

the newspaper. "'Witnesses Spot Princess in Tokyo! Two London residents were on holiday Thursday in Japan, where they claim to have seen Princess Eliana, missing since last week, in a Tokyo bathhouse.'"

"That's preposterous!" Portia exclaimed. "What would the youngest daughter of the Queen of England be doing in Tokyo?"

"Taking a bath, apparently," Lina said dryly.

"Does the article cite any evidence?" Portia asked in her elegant, cultured accent.

"No, that's the odd part," said Emily. "The article goes on to quote the police as saying the witnesses were probably mistaken. There's no proof at all! My internship may be with BBC television instead of a newspaper, but I know enough about newspapers to know this is shoddy journalism. What were the editors thinking, to run such a dicey story on page one?"

"I suppose they were thinking, 'This article will sell a lot of newspapers,'" Portia remarked.

Lina reached for the *Journal* and ruffled through it. "Here's an advertisement for your play, Portia!" she exclaimed in her charming Liverpudlian accent. "Listen to this: 'Young Penelope Abbott, playing the part of Isabelle, is the most exciting thing to hit the London stage since Felicity Kendall.' That's just super, Portia! I'm sorry I couldn't go with everyone on Thursday night. I can't wait to see it."

Emily laughed. "I'm not surprised about your rave reviews. You practiced the part of stuck-up Isabelle Huntington so diligently, twenty-four hours a day, that we all believed you were an insufferable snob! I've heard of dedication, but even an

7

actress has to be at leisure now and then."

"Once again, I do apologize," Portia said, with a formal bow. "I don't know how you all ever forgave me. I really got carried away."

Lina laughed. "We're just thankful you weren't rehearsing for the part of Jack the Ripper!"

"It's too bad you can't use your real name in the cast," Emily said. "Have you called your father in Scotland yet to tell him that you landed a role? I would think he'd be pleased that you want to follow in his footsteps. Maybe someday, you'll be as famous an actor as he is."

"No, I haven't told him," Portia said. "And I'm not sure I will. I told you—the venerable Sir Montford Albert disapproves of my ambition to be an actress. He claims it's too hard a life, and he's not certain I have the talent to make a go of it. That's why I haven't told him I got this role, and why I'm using the stage name Penelope Abbott. I had to learn what I'm capable of, on my own. I couldn't let my father's name influence people's reactions to my work."

"Sometimes you have to get away from your past before you can find out who you really are," Lina said thoughtfully. Emily stared at her curiously. She liked Lina a lot, but sometimes the girl from Liverpool said the oddest things.

Portia didn't seem to think it was odd. "Then I guess I've learned that I am an actress," she said. "I still don't know if I've any real talent, but I do know that it's all I've ever wanted to do. Now that I know what it's like to be onstage in a professional production, I want to act more than ever. I just hope I can someday con-

8

vince my father and make him proud of me."

"You will," Lina said staunchly.

"Well, speaking of being an actress," Portia said, rising from her chair, "I have to get to rehearsal."

"Break a leg," Emily called as she left the room. "That is the expression, isn't it?"

Emily had plenty of faith in Portia's talent. But she thought the conversation had become much too serious. "I miss the American twins," she said suddenly. "This place was much jollier with them around."

Lina smiled. "Yes, it certainly was."

Emily sighed jealously. "It's bad enough that Jess and Liz are gorgeous and nice. But within a few days of arriving in the country, Jessica snagged a real English nobleman! It's not fair!"

"Robert Pembroke *is* one of the most eligible guys in London," Lina admitted.

"And Elizabeth hooked up with that cute, sensitive Luke, from the *Journal*—not to mention the torch that Rene Glize is carrying for her! The best-looking boy at HIS! Who could have guessed that he knew the twins from their trip to France? And now he's here working for the French Embassy!

"Face it, Lina," she concluded, "coincidences like that only happen to people like Jessica and Elizabeth. They obviously lead charmed lives—unlike normal, everyday blokes like you and me."

Lina smiled enigmatically.

"Of course," Emily continued in her characteristic nonstop fashion, "it's a shame that Rene is jealous of Luke and has been giving Liz the cold shoulder all week."

9

"I know," Lina said. "Liz just wants to be friends with Rene, so he won't even talk to her."

Emily sighed. "Until Rene gets over Liz, he's no good as potential boyfriend material. So—except for Gabriello Moretti, who already has a girlfriend—it seems that the twins, between them, have tied up all the good-looking guys around!"

"Not all of them," Lina pointed out.

Emily smiled. "David Bartholomew, right?"

"Am I that transparent?" Lina blushed.

"You're so honest, Lina, that you couldn't keep a secret if your life depended on it. Everybody at HIS knows that you and David are crazy about each other. We're ready to take wagers on when you'll finally give in to all that passion and go out on a date. So when's it going to be?"

Lina blushed again. "Tonight," she said. "Liz finally convinced me that I should, as the Americans say, go for it."

"Liz would know," Emily says. "Look where she and her sister are right now—guests of Pembroke Manor! I bet they're having a fantastic time. . . ."

A half hour after Joy's body was found, Jessica sat next to Robert on an overstuffed sofa in the Pembrokes' parlor, drinking a cup of tea. Now that she was away from the bedroom and those bloody sheets, the murder hardly seemed real. She leaned against Robert's shoulder and put the gory scene out of her mind, concentrating instead on the excitement of being in the middle of a real English murder mystery—just like in an Agatha Christie book.

10

The sumptuous furnishings and aristocratic people around her were pretty exciting, too. Jessica thought of Lila Fowler, her best friend back home in California. Lila was the daughter of a millionaire, but even Lila wasn't related to royalty, like the Pembrokes. She would be green with envy when she heard about the people Jessica was hanging out with.

The Pembroke family, their staff, and the weekend guests were assembled in the parlor for questioning by the local authorities. Thin, regal Lady Pembroke was sitting, ramrod straight, on the edge of an upholstered chair. Even at this hour of the morning, Jessica marveled, she was perfectly coiffed and made up. Lord Pembroke was nervously pacing back and forth across the thick oriental carpeting.

But it was their son Robert to whom Jessica's thoughts kept returning. She loved his classy, English clothing and his handsome face. But she was even more impressed by his confident manner, and how he took command of every situation. At the murder scene earlier today, the others had stared at the body in shock. But Robert had known exactly what to do. He had set the servants in motion and instructed everyone to meet down here to wait for the authorities. Now she snuggled against his strong body, feeling safe and secure.

Elizabeth and Luke huddled together on a sofa that faced the one Jessica sat on. Elizabeth, as usual, held a small notebook in her hand. *Leave it to my twin*, Jessica thought. *She never can give those reporter's instincts a rest*. Elizabeth was scribbling wildly in her notebook, stopping only when she noticed the police constable's unfriendly glare.

Constable Sheila Atherton, a small, dark-haired woman in her mid-thirties, stood near the sofa, looming over Elizabeth in a way that made her look much larger than her short stature.

"You say that you and your sister are from a village called Sweet Valley, California?" she asked in a no-nonsense voice. Thunder crashed outside the window, punctuating the constable's question and whipping the light morning drizzle into a downpour.

Village? Jessica thought. *How very English.* Frequently, she found herself annoyed and mystified by the unfamiliar words she'd been hearing in England. British English and American English were very different languages, she was learning. But in this setting—the parlor of a British manor house— words like "village" seemed absolutely right. She would have to get Robert to teach her how to talk that way.

"That's right," Elizabeth answered the constable's question. "We're in London for a summer internship, and the Pembrokes invited us to spend the weekend here."

The constable drained her teacup and set it on the table with a loud clank. "Dawn was hardly a civilized hour to be roaming about the corridors this morning, Ms. Wakefield. How did you happen to discover the body?"

"I was worried that Jessica might be in danger," Elizabeth explained, "so I ran down the hall to her room and saw . . . the victim."

12

Lord Pembroke, still pacing, wheeled abruptly, nearly crashing into the tall, thin man who was carrying in a tea tray. Pembroke sat down quickly in a straight-backed chair as the servant righted the tray and carried it to the table in front of the constable. Jessica heard the silver serving pieces clinking together; the servant's hands were trembling. Apparently, the murder had set the whole household's nerves on edge.

The constable poured herself a second cup of tea. "But *why* were you worried, Ms. Wakefield? What would make you suddenly believe your sister was in danger?"

Elizabeth blushed. "It may sound silly, but I had a nightmare about it."

The constable raised her eyebrows.

"And when I woke up," Elizabeth continued staunchly, "I just knew there was something wrong."

Jessica spoke up helpfully. "It happens to us all the time. It's because we're identical twins."

"Oh, really?" the constable asked sarcastically, taking in the girls' identical heart-shaped faces, blue-green eyes, and slim, athletic figures. Even their California suntans were exactly the same shade, though they were starting to fade after a week in foggy England. "I hadn't noticed."

Thatcher rose from his chair, an imposing figure, even in his grief. "What did you do when you entered the room, Elizabeth?" he asked in a tightly controlled voice.

Constable Atherton cast the police chief a dark look. "With all due respect, sir, this is not London," she reminded him. "And we are out of your jurisdiction. *I* am conducting this investigation, if you don't mind."

Andrew turned his back on her and stared instead at the rain-soaked gardens outside the window.

Elizabeth glanced over at him, her eyes full of sympathy. Then she took a deep breath and spoke to the constable. "I walked into the room and saw . . . everything. . . . It was Jessica's bed, so I thought it was Jessica. I guess I started screaming. Then Luke came running in. A minute later, Jessica showed up."

The constable turned to Luke. "And why were *you* roaming the halls at sunrise, young man?"

"I wasn't," he said quietly. "I was having trouble sleeping. I heard Elizabeth scream, so I ran out of my room to find her."

Lord Pembroke spoke up suddenly. "I hardly see that this line of questioning is leading anywhere!" he said in his booming voice. "You don't honestly believe that this girl is the murderer, do you?"

"I admit it's unlikely," the constable replied evenly. "But everybody is a suspect." She glared at him thoughtfully. "And I do mean everybody."

Lord Pembroke seemed awfully nervous, Elizabeth noticed as the family patriarch sat down. Of course, anyone would be jumpy, after what had happened in Jessica's room that night. But Elizabeth thought his reaction seemed extreme—especially coming from a man so accustomed to affecting the cool, superior demeanor of the British aristocracy.

Elizabeth wrote a line in her notebook: *"Keep an eye on the elder Pembroke."*

She gazed around the room again, thankful that the constable seemed to be finished with her for now.

Everybody in the room was a suspect, the constable had said. So who else appeared to be hiding something? Elizabeth gazed thoughtfully at the servants. Tall, thin Alistair had seemed friendly and innocuous when she had met him the day before. She could hardly believe he was a killer. But she had noticed his hands shaking as he set down the tea tray. Why? Maybe he knew more than he was saying.

Alistair whispered something to Maria Finch, the Pembrokes' pretty, plump cook. She stared at the rich red carpeting, wringing her hands; Elizabeth was afraid the woman would burst into tears. Was Maria hiding something, as well? Elizabeth resolved to question the two servants herself, later.

"Alistair," a calm, commanding voice reproached suddenly. "You forgot the lemon." Elizabeth focused thoughtfully on young Robert Pembroke, who sat with his arm around Jessica.

Alistair bowed apologetically. "I beg your pardon, sir," he said. "I'll fetch it right away." He turned on his heel and disappeared through the double doors.

Elizabeth shook her head disapprovingly. Ever since she'd come to Pembroke Manor, she'd been annoyed by the way the Pembrokes treated the "lower" classes. She had never heard a "please" or a "thank you" out of Robert; he took it for granted that people would cater to his every whim. She hated his commanding tone and bossy manners.

Now, Elizabeth had to admit, Robert had a concerned expression on his face, especially when he looked at Jessica. But unlike his father and the servants, Robert didn't seem nervous. In fact, he looked particularly cool and regal. Somehow, he—like his parents—had found time in the last twenty minutes to dress fully; his cravat was expertly tied and his dark hair was combed. Robert was handsome, certainly. And Jessica was crazy about him. Still, Elizabeth couldn't stand his smug, superior way of looking down his nose at people. Of course, that didn't make him an animalistic murderer.

"We all have an animal side," she found herself writing in the notebook. For a moment, the sentence startled her, as if someone else had written it there. Then she remembered Luke using those words earlier in the week, as he and Elizabeth toured the eerie werewolf exhibit at the wax museum in London. *We all have an animal side.* As much as Elizabeth hated to admit it, she had to agree—especially after what had happened early Saturday morning.

Thank goodness for sweet, gentle Luke, Elizabeth thought, feeling the warmth of his fisherman's sweater against her shoulder. The young poet was becoming more important to her with every passing day, making it disturbingly easy to put out of her mind the image of Todd Wilkins, her boyfriend back in California.

In fact, to Elizabeth, sitting in the parlor of an English manor house the morning after a murder, California seemed like another planet altogether.

She was startled out of her thoughts by Constable

16

Atherton, who wheeled abruptly to face Jessica.

"A girl was murdered last night in the bed you were supposed to be sleeping in!" the constable reminded Jessica. "Tell me, Ms. Wakefield, who might want you dead?"

Jessica shrugged her shoulders comically. "Well, there's Lila Fowler, but she's still back in Sweet Valley. Other than her, I can't imagine!"

Elizabeth smiled. She could always count on Jessica to cover up her anxiety with a joke.

The constable's eyes narrowed. "This is a serious situation, Ms. Wakefield. Do you have any enemies?"

Jessica rolled her eyes, and Elizabeth realized she wasn't covering up her fear—she wasn't afraid at all. *She doesn't take any of this seriously,* Elizabeth realized with dismay. *She thinks she's the star of an Agatha Christie play.*

Jessica shrugged her shoulders. "I'm one of the most popular people in my town, and I hardly know anyone within about a million miles of here. Besides, I'm only six—" She stopped and glanced at Robert. "I'm only a teenager," she concluded.

Elizabeth sighed, realizing that Jessica must be pretending to Robert that she was older than sixteen. *Leave it to Jessica to be worried about keeping a rich, handsome twenty-year-old interested in her—even with a murderer on the loose.*

"Face it," Jessica said to the room full of people. "I couldn't have been the target. Nobody would want me dead. It was just a random murder, like that doctor who was killed in London last week, and the nurse before that."

The chief of police turned from the window and stared at Jessica curiously. Elizabeth held her breath. *Leave it to Jessica to open her big mouth!* Nobody was supposed to know that the girls had been at the Essex Street murder scene. And only someone who had been there—and seen the body— would make the connection between Dr. Neville's death and Joy Singleton's. And no information had been released about a connection to the death of a nurse the month before—despite the fact that the police must have noticed similarities between the cases. Somebody—or something—had ripped out the nurse's throat, too.

For some reason, *London Journal* editor Henry Reeves had not printed the details of the doctor's death. Lucy Friday had been crime desk editor at the time, and she had quit her job over the decision. Jessica and Elizabeth were determined to find out why Reeves—or the *Journal*'s owner, Lord Pembroke himself—would cover up such important news. But now Jessica may have tipped their hands.

Andrew opened his mouth to question Jessica, but Lord Pembroke beat him to it. The older man jumped from his chair again, knocking it over with a clatter.

"What do you mean, Miss Wakefield?" Lord Pembroke asked sharply. "Why would you compare last night's slaying to the death of Cameron Neville?"

Jessica glanced apologetically at Elizabeth. Then she smiled at Lord Pembroke. "That's just what I meant," she explained sweetly. "Both were completely random incidents. There is no connection."

18

"Let's stick to the facts of the case at hand, please," the constable insisted. "Ms. Wakefield, at approximately what time did Ms. Singleton come to your room?"

Jessica shrugged. "Sorry, but keeping track of the time isn't one of my strong points," she said. "I don't even wear a watch in the daytime—let alone in the middle of the night."

The constable's expression was venomous. "Could you hazard a guess?"

Jessica shrugged again. "I don't know—two or three o'clock in the morning, I suppose."

The constable turned around slowly, staring, in turn, at every person in the room. "Was anyone else awake this morning between two o'clock and, shall we say, five o'clock?"

Elizabeth shook her head quickly and saw that most of the others did, too. But she noticed that Maria looked down at the floor, blushing as red as the expensive oriental carpet that covered it.

The constable noticed too. "Ms. Finch, may I remind you that this is an official police investigation? Were you awake at that time this morning?"

Maria nodded slowly, still looking down. "Yes, ma'am," she replied, barely above a whisper. Alistair had returned to the room a few minutes earlier, with a dish of lemon wedges for the tea. Now he stood beside Maria, and she clutched his arm tightly as she spoke.

"I'm always up and about early," Maria stammered, "to prepare the morning meal, you know." She paused, a frightened look on her face. "But I didn't see a thing, ma'am. I swear it. I was mostly in the kitchen, anyways."

The constable glared at her suspiciously. "Very well," she said at last. "I suppose you can all go about your business, for now. But don't anyone leave the country without first notifying my office."

As the group began filing out of the parlor in the direction of the dining room, Luke leaned over to whisper in Elizabeth's ear. "Doesn't it seem odd to you that we're calmly preparing to eat brunch, just hours after a murder?"

Elizabeth nodded. "You know how these Pembrokes are caught up in tradition," she whispered back. "If the custom is to eat brunch on Saturdays, they certainly wouldn't let a little thing like a murder get in the way."

Out of the corner of her eye, she noticed Lord Pembroke tap Andrew Thatcher on the shoulder as if asking him to stay behind in the parlor.

"You go on with the rest," Elizabeth whispered to Luke. "I'll catch up with you in a minute."

Elizabeth turned back to the parlor and peered into the room, around the edge of the open door. The two men stood facing the window, their backs to her. Elizabeth felt a twinge of conscience about eaves-dropping, but put it out of her mind as Lord Pembroke began to speak.

The older man patted Thatcher's shoulder in a paternal manner. "Just a little more time, Andrew," he said. "It's too good an opportunity to pass up—"

Thatcher whirled to face him. "But Joy—"

"You know how sorry I am about your young lady, Thatcher. But it doesn't change anything. This is still the chance of a lifetime. We only have to hold on a little longer."

Andrew turned back to the window and nodded, almost imperceptibly. Elizabeth had to strain to hear his next words. "All right, Robert. As you wish."

Lord Pembroke steered the younger man toward the door. Elizabeth darted behind it and scrunched her body against the wall, scribbling down everything they had said. Then she followed them down the hall, keeping what she hoped was a safe distance as she pretended to admire the paintings of stern-looking relatives who stared accusingly from the richly brocaded walls.

Constable Atherton met the two men at the end of the hallway. "Gentlemen," she said in a low voice. "I have been thinking about the comment young Ms. Wakefield made concerning the unfortunate incidents in London. You must be involved in that investigation, Chief Thatcher. Do you believe there is any connection?"

There was a pause before Andrew's voice answered. "No, Constable. I honestly do not believe there is a connection between the two deaths in London, or between those deaths and this one. There is no evidence to support such a link."

Elizabeth's eyes widened. As the threesome disappeared into the dining room, she struggled to copy down Thatcher's exact words, incredulous that the police would lie about the fact that three murders had been committed in exactly the same gruesome manner. *Four* murders, she corrected herself, thinking about poor Poo-Poo, the Yorkshire terrier. The story of Poo-Poo's disappearance had been the twins' first assignment for the *Journal.* The case had seemed insignificant at first, but it had taken on a chilling tone when Elizabeth found the little dog's lifeless body on a London street corner Monday night, its throat torn open.

Elizabeth scribbled one more line in her notebook: *"Who is Thatcher trying to protect?"*

Suddenly, a strong hand locked on Elizabeth's wrist. She jumped, slamming the notebook shut.

Lord Pembroke's voice sounded in her ear, calm, but with what Elizabeth thought was a note of menace. "I've seen you writing in that tablet of yours," he said. "Don't entertain any grand ideas about getting your byline in the paper with any of this. The young woman's death is of no interest in London. It's local news. That's all."

He dropped her wrist abruptly and glided to the other end of the room, not looking back.

Elizabeth flushed guiltily. She *had* been imagining her byline on page one of the *London Journal*— on an article that covered something more important than an exploding eggplant or a missing dog, which were the kinds of stories she'd been assigned all week. Of course, Pembroke owned the *Journal.* If he really was covering up information about the murders, her chances of exposing him in the newspaper were slim. Still, she was determined to learn the truth.

She turned back to her first page of notes and underlined a sentence: *"Keep an eye on the elder Pembroke."*

She studied him as he stood with Robert, Jessica, and an uncomfortable-looking Luke. *Poor, sensitive Luke!* He hated being around rich, snobby types even more than Elizabeth did, but he had come to spend the weekend here because Elizabeth had asked him to.

Now Luke was staring, eyes narrowed, at both Pembrokes, as Jessica carried on what appeared to be an animated monologue. The Pembrokes ignored Luke completely. Robert's eyes never left Jessica's face, and even Lord Pembroke seemed to relax, caught in the spell of Jessica's vivacity.

Elizabeth noticed that the dining room was decorated with safari trophies. From the wall over Jessica's head, a tiger's mouth gaped open, its dagger-like teeth glistening in the morning sunlight.

A sense of dark foreboding washed over Elizabeth, and she felt as if she were drowning. And again she heard Luke's words in her mind, so clearly that she almost turned to see if he was standing beside her, whispering in her ear:

We all have an animal side.

Chapter 2

"Thanks for the snack, Maria," Elizabeth said, sitting at the worktable in the huge kitchen of Pembroke Manor. "Your homemade cookies—I mean, *biscuits*— are first-rate."

"Oh, it's no bother at all, Miss Wakefield," the plump, pretty cook replied.

"I guess I wasn't feeling very hungry at brunch," Elizabeth said carefully, "after what happened this morning."

Maria turned away quickly, but not until after Elizabeth caught a frightened look in her brown eyes. Once again, she was certain that the cook knew more about Joy's murder than she had told the constable.

Alistair walked into the kitchen, carrying a dust rag, and Elizabeth noticed the familiar way he rested a hand on Maria's shoulder as he leaned over to whisper something in her ear. She smiled up at him gratefully, as if he'd offered words of encouragement.

Maria wasn't the only person who was grateful for Alistair's presence. Elizabeth wanted to question both of them, somewhere out of earshot of the Pembrokes. Now was her chance.

"Would you care for more biscuits—I mean, *cookies*—miss?" Maria asked.

"No, thank you, Maria. Actually, I wanted to talk with both of you for a moment. About last night."

Maria's face turned white, and Alistair began clasping and unclasping his hands.

"As I told the constable, miss," Maria said, "I was awake at the time, but I didn't see a thing near Miss Jessica's room."

Interesting, Elizabeth thought. *I didn't mention Jessica's room.* And Maria had implied to the constable that she'd been only in the kitchen that morning.

"I heard what you said to the constable," Elizabeth replied carefully. "I was just wondering if you'd remembered anything else since you talked to her."

Maria stared at the linoleum. "Not a thing, miss."

"I know what it's like to be awake, in the dark, when everyone else is asleep," Elizabeth began slowly. "Sometimes you hear noises, and they scare you, but you tell yourself it was only the house settling, or the wind rattling the gutters. Did either of you hear anything like that this morning?"

Alistair's hands were trembling again.

"Alistair, the constable never asked you directly. Were you awake at all between two and five this morning?"

He sat down limply at the worktable. "We would like to oblige you, miss," he said in a tense whisper, "but we mustn't. We could lose our positions if Lord Pembroke were to find out."

So that was it. They were terrified of their employer. The realization made Elizabeth even more determined to discover exactly what Pembroke's role was in all of this. *What was he hiding?* She knew she would have to proceed slowly with Alistair and Maria.

"Somebody is trying to cover up the facts of some murders here and in London," Elizabeth said. "I'm investigating to find out the truth. I won't tell anyone you spoke to me."

"You won't tell young Master Pembroke?" Maria asked.

"Maria, no!" Alistair begged. "It's too dangerous."

"Please, Alistair. A young woman is dead. If we can help Miss Wakefield find the killer—" She hesitated.

"Nobody will ever know you talked to me," Elizabeth assured her. "A good journalist never reveals her sources."

Maria swallowed hard and then began to speak haltingly. "The moon was full last night," she said, "and Alistair and I crept out for a romantic walk in the gardens, an hour before I was to begin the morning's work in the kitchen. Of course, we stayed quite close to the house, what with the poor sheep that were found dead, and all. We had just come inside, around about four o'clock, and were at the end of the upstairs corridor."

"We had come upstairs for clean table linens for the morning meal," Alistair interjected, drumming his fingers nervously on the wooden table. "We planned to bring them down the servants' stairway at the end of the hall, and—"

"And somebody was in the hallway leaving Miss Jessica's room!" Maria blurted out.

Elizabeth felt the hair rise on the back of her neck. "Who was it?" she asked breathlessly.

"I heard footsteps in the hallway—" Alistair admitted.

"Alistair didn't see the person," Maria said. "Only me. He already had the stairway door open and was about to head down the steps. Of course, it was very dark," she added. "I really couldn't tell who it was in the corridor."

"Can you give me any information at all about the person you saw?" Elizabeth asked. "Hair color? Height? Clothing?"

Maria shook her head and refused to meet Elizabeth's gaze. Tears glistened in her dark eyes. Now more than ever, Elizabeth was sure Maria knew—or could guess at—the identity of the person in the hallway. But she was obviously too frightened to say more.

"It was very dark," Maria repeated.

"It's awfully early for it to be so dark." Jessica clasped Robert's hand tighter, as if she were frightened by the drifting English mist in the boxwood garden.

It was twilight on Saturday. Except for anguished Andrew Thatcher, who had driven back to London after brunch, the guests at Pembroke Manor had spent a quiet day indoors, recovering from the morning's horror and avoiding a torrential downpour that had finally stopped late in the afternoon.

Jessica wasn't really cold, but she shivered. Robert draped his strong arm around her shoulders, which is just what she had wanted him to do.

"We can go back inside, if you'd like," he said. "I know you've suffered a terrible shock. It's beastly of me to keep you out in this sort of weather."

"Oh, no!" Jessica said. "It feels good to get out in the fresh air after being cooped up inside with everyone all afternoon—even if it's so misty I can hardly see the garden! Besides, I feel perfectly safe, with you. I know you would never let anything hurt me."

Robert smiled down at her, and Jessica felt her knees turn to jelly. He was definitely the best-looking guy she had ever dated. And being fabulously wealthy—and part of the British aristocracy—didn't hurt. Despite the damp weather, Jessica suddenly felt warm under his gaze.

"You poor girl. You're still unsteady. I'm horribly sorry you've had to endure such trauma while a visitor at my home. I suppose it doesn't say much for the Pembroke hospitality."

"Oh, Robert. It's not your family's fault that such an awful thing happened to poor Joy. And just because it happened in my own bed doesn't mean I'm frightened or anything."

Of course, Jessica admitted to herself, she had been frightened at first. Now she felt completely recovered, but there was no reason to act like she was—not when he was being so attentive. Traumatic experiences had their uses.

"You are so brave, Jessica," he said, squeezing her hand. "I'm proud of you. Even *I* am feeling a bit troubled about the situation—a murder has taken place in my own home! But you are determined not to let it spoil everyone's weekend."

Jessica smiled shyly. "Robert, I want you to know how much I appreciate your invitation to visit your family's beautiful country home." She gestured around the garden, knowing that sculpted hedges and tasteful flower beds hid beneath the shroud of mist. "Despite what happened to Joy, I've had a great time this weekend—with you."

He frowned. "I'm just sorry it's about to end. Do you have to take the first train in the morning?"

"Well," Jessica pretended to hesitate, "Elizabeth *is* a real stickler when it comes to punctuality. . . ."

Robert grinned. "I've got an idea. Allow me to make it up to you for the horrendous weekend. I know this smashing restaurant in Windsor. It takes weeks for most people to get reservations, but the owner is a friend of my family's. I'll arrange a table for tonight. In the morning, you can sleep as long as you like, and I'll drive you back to London at your leisure. How does that sound?"

"Heavenly," Jessica declared, thinking of an evening alone with Robert—and his luxurious silver Jaguar convertible. "You know, I really could get used to this lifestyle, Robert. You always seem to get the best and the nicest of everything!"

Robert stared into her eyes. "You deserve nothing but the best and the nicest."

Then he leaned over and pressed his warm, soft lips against hers. A warm tingling spread through Jessica's body as she returned his slow, ardent kiss.

Afterward, she stood for a few minutes in Robert's arms, breathing the heady scent of his cologne and gazing over his shoulder at the wisps of fog that drifted across the yellow face of the moon.

Late that night, Elizabeth stood in the dark corridor outside the door of the room that Joy Singleton had died in. She looked down the long, dim hallway in both directions and then breathed a sigh of relief. It was empty.

The train for London would leave first thing in the morning, so this could be Elizabeth's last chance to search for clues. Robert and Jessica were out for a late dinner in nearby Cambridge. The Pembrokes and their servants had gone to bed, or were busy in other parts of the great house. Andrew Thatcher had returned to London that afternoon. And Luke was in his room, studying the werewolf lore that had always been a hobby for him, but had lately become an obsession.

Elizabeth felt a pang of guilt at investigating Joy's death without letting Luke know. After all, they were in this together. It wasn't that she wanted to keep secrets from him, exactly. But Luke was so convinced about his werewolf theory that Elizabeth was afraid he wouldn't keep an open mind about any clues they might discover.

"Of course," she said under her breath, "Luke may be right. It just might be a werewolf. But a good journalist has to consider every possibility."

She entered the room and quietly pulled the door shut behind her. "Clues," she said aloud. But where should she look for them?

31

The crime had taken place on the bed, of course. Elizabeth's heart began pounding as she approached it. The scene was there before her: the body that looked like Jessica's . . . the golden hair . . . the crimson blood that soaked into the sheets and dripped steadily into a small pool on the parquet floor.

She shook her head to clear it of the image. Of course, the bed was empty now, cold and bare of linens. The only sign that remained of the morning's crime was a round reddish-brown stain on the floor beside the bed.

Clearly, no clues were left on the bare mattress. She scanned the tastefully furnished room. An armoire stood in one corner, its doors wide open to reveal an empty interior. No doubt it had already been searched by the police. Of course, the police must have searched the entire room. But they might have missed something, Elizabeth told herself. Something important.

She traced what might be the murderer's footsteps. The killer must have entered through the door, walked across the rug to the bed, murdered Joy, and skulked out—to be seen by Maria Finch, who had been standing near the door to the servants' stairs at the far end of the hallway.

Elizabeth peered at the rug that covered much of the floor. There was no trace of the killer's having crossed it—not that Elizabeth had really expected to find any.

"What else in the room did the murderer touch?" she asked herself. Then she realized she was staring at the answer. The door.

Elizabeth inspected the shiny brass door handle. As expected, she found nothing. The constable's assistant had dusted it for fingerprints that morning, and the servants had polished it carefully afterward, to remove the powdery black dust.

"What's this?" she whispered, running her hand up and down the wooden door frame. Caught in a crack in the wood were some silky threads from some kind of dark-green fabric. At last, she had found some evidence.

But there was more. She pulled a small wad of a wiry material out of the crack. Chills raced up and down her spine as she realized what she was holding in her hand.

It was a piece of animal fur, with long, coarse hairs.

The applause was over; the curtain had closed on Saturday night's performance of *A Common Man*. But the biggest standing ovation yet was still ringing in Portia's ears as she stood backstage, tired but exhilarated.

She felt a small hand clasp her shoulder. "Great work, Penelope!" said tiny, dark-haired Adrian Rani, a cast member who was about Portia's age. "That was your best performance yet!"

After chatting for a moment, Adrian walked to the stage door, where a beaming middle-aged couple waited for her. Portia sighed as she watched Adrian embrace her parents.

"What's the sigh for, Portia—or should I say, Penelope?" asked a voice behind her.

"Rene!" Portia exclaimed, glad to see the tall, handsome French boy. "How did you like the performance?"

"The play was *tres bon*—excellent. And you were even better. I am pleased that I was finally able to see it. But why did you sigh so sadly?"

Portia smiled. "Oh, I do feel great about tonight's show. I just wish my parents could be here and feeling great about it, too. Without my father's support, even the standing ovations seem empty."

"So, invite your papa to tomorrow's show."

Portia bit her lip. "You know, my father is actually here in London at the moment. He arrived today from Scotland for a meeting with the Royal Shakespeare Company." Then she sighed and shook her head. "But it's not that easy, Rene. You know how he feels about my chances of making it as an actress."

"The important thing, Portia, is this: How do you feel about your chances of making it as an actress?"

"I don't know," Portia said, biting her lip. "Maybe my father's right. Anyone can get lucky in one little play. Perhaps I don't have enough talent to make a career of acting."

"And perhaps you do. Personally, I believe you must. Only an actress *par excellence* could have created the illusion that you created at HIS in the last few weeks. You portrayed Isabelle so well that we all—as Jessica would say—*hated your guts!* Only now can I truly understand why you were being such a royal pain in the neck." He laughed. "But after seeing you in action tonight, I think I can forgive you."

Portia blushed under her heavy stage makeup. "I know I was beastly to everyone, Rene. Playing a role is no excuse for that kind of behavior. I'm glad you can forgive me for it." She stared him straight in the eye. "But now can you forgive Liz, as well?"

Rene flinched. "Ah, Portia. Let's not bring that up. I loved Elizabeth. She was everything I could ever want in a girl, but she betrayed—"

"No, she didn't betray you," Portia protested. "You and Elizabeth didn't have a relationship when she started seeing Luke."

Rene forced a laugh. "Come now, Portia. Hasn't anyone ever told you it's presumptuous for a *Brit* to advise a *Frenchman* on matters of love?"

Portia shook her head. "Oh, no. You are absolutely not going to extract yourself from this conversation by trying to engage me in Franco-English sparring. I'm quite fond of Elizabeth. She was the only person who made an effort to befriend me at first—even while I was treating everyone so abominably." She folded her arms. "Rene, before the Wakefields arrived in London, you hadn't set eyes on Elizabeth in months. Isn't it a wee bit possible that you've fallen in love with a memory, rather than a real person?"

"She didn't allow me to get reacquainted with the real person!" Rene protested. "She had hardly stepped off the plane when she began keeping company with that . . . *poet*."

"You make 'poet' sound like a dirty word."

"I can't help it. I love her. I don't want to see her with another beau."

"If you love Liz, you should want her to be happy. And she seems happy with Luke. Don't spoil that for her."

35

"But she said she cared for me."

"She does," Portia assured him. "Your friendship is very important to Elizabeth right now. And who knows what might happen in the future? If you can't be her mate—I mean, *friend*—now, you'll lose her completely, forever."

Rene cocked his head. "I don't know, Portia. I'm not sure I could handle being 'mates' with Elizabeth—especially if I have to watch her swooning over Luke Shepherd's poetry. But I suppose you've given me something to think about."

"Good," Portia said. "Now, let's think about stopping somewhere for a bite to eat. I'll introduce you to the old English standby, fish and chips."

Rene grimaced. "Hasn't anyone ever told you it's presumptuous for a Brit to advise a Frenchman on matters of *food*?"

"How did Jessica enjoy her date last night with Little Lord Pembroke?" Luke asked Elizabeth, who sat beside him on the Sunday morning train back to London.

"I don't know," Elizabeth said. "She was still asleep when we left this morning. I suppose she had a wonderful time, but I'm worried about her. I don't think Robert Pembroke is the right kind of guy for her. I've heard he's led kind of a wild life. What do you know about him?"

Luke narrowed his eyes. "Quite a bit, actually. His father tries to quell the gossip, but the Pembrokes are the sort of people everyone adores talking about. Robert has been booted out of some of the finest schools in Britain. He's known for his attendance at the wildest parties And he drives that Jaguar of his like a bloody maniac. In addition, his picture is in the tabloids every fortnight or so with a different female companion hanging on to his arm or gazing adoringly into his wealthy, aristocratic eyes. What do girls like Jessica see in his type?"

"Jessica's never been a very good judge of character," Elizabeth admitted. "In fact, we never like the same people. She's not a bad person, Luke, but she gets carried away. She places too much importance on appearances."

Luke touched Elizabeth's cheek for a brief, exquisite moment. "And appearances, as we know, can be deceiving," he replied in the soft, lilting accent that made everything he said sound like poetry. "I'm glad you're so different from your twin sister—despite your identical appearances."

"And *I'm* glad that you're nothing like Robert Pembroke," Elizabeth asserted. Her cheek felt warm where Luke had touched it.

"In one area, Robert has me topped," Luke admitted. "He took his girlfriend out last night, while I remained cloistered in my room, reading about werewolf imagery in Native-American rites and rituals. I hope you weren't too lonely, on your own."

Elizabeth pulled an envelope out of her backpack, and handed it to him. "Actually, I was busy last night," she said, unable to conceal her excitement. "Look what I found in the door frame of the room where Joy was murdered."

Luke twisted the green threads in his fingers.

"Fibers from some sort of fabric—it looks like silk." His eyes widened. "And this is animal fur!"

Elizabeth nodded, feeling every bit like Nancy Drew. "When we find out where those green threads come from, we'll be much closer to identifying the murderer."

"And the fur proves that it's a werewolf!"

"It doesn't *necessarily prove* anything," Elizabeth argued, trying to remember that first and foremost she was a journalist. "We don't know for sure what that fur comes from."

"We most certainly do!" Luke insisted. "What else but a werewolf could have murdered Joy Singleton by ripping her throat open? Not to mention the London victims. The question is, who is the werewolf?"

"I'm still not sure I believe in werewolves, but I'm willing to accept the possibility."

"Are you familiar with the words of your American poet, Thoreau?" Luke asked. "'The moon now rises to her absolute rule. And the husbandman and the hunter acknowledge her as their mistress.' The werewolf is the ultimate hunter, Elizabeth. He can change shape whenever he's so moved, but when the full moon shines, he's at his greatest strength. And the full moon was shining on the night of Joy's death."

Elizabeth suppressed a shudder. "Well, whether the murderer is a werewolf or not, the constable said everyone is a suspect. So let's go over all the possibilities. Who could have killed Joy Singleton?"

Luke counted on his fingers. "Besides Joy, the only people at Pembroke Manor this weekend were

38

you and me, Jessica, the three Pembrokes, the servants, and Andrew Thatcher. I guess we can safely say it wasn't you, me, or Jessica."

Elizabeth nodded. "Right. And I can't believe Thatcher could have killed Joy. He was in love with her."

"Agreed," Luke said. "That leaves the Pembrokes and the servants. You questioned Maria and Alistair. What's your opinion about them?"

"I don't think they're murderers," Elizabeth said thoughtfully. "But they were in the upstairs hallway around the time of the murder. And I'm sure they're hiding something. Maria saw someone—or something—in the hallway outside of the room where Joy was killed. She says she doesn't know who it was. I think she's lying."

"Interesting. What about Alistair?"

Elizabeth shook her head. "I don't believe he saw anything. I'm not sure if Maria told him who she thinks she saw, but I know he's afraid to let her talk about it."

"Who are they afraid of?"

"Pembroke," Elizabeth replied. "The elder Lord Pembroke, that is. They were terrified that he would find out they spoke with me."

"Pembroke again," Luke said. "And the only suspects we haven't eliminated are Lord Pembroke, Lady Pembroke, and Robert. It must be one of them."

"We can't accuse someone of murder based only on the process of elimination," Elizabeth reminded him. "The Pembrokes could be innocent. Maybe we're wrong about one of the other suspects. Maybe there was some other servant in the house that night. Or maybe someone we've never heard of broke into the house and murdered Joy."

"Do you honestly believe that, Liz?"

Elizabeth hesitated before shaking her head. "No. I guess I agree that the Pembrokes are our prime suspects. But we can't do anything about it until we have some firm evidence that implicates one of them."

"We'll find the evidence," Luke assured her. "Werewolves are expert killers. But they aren't terribly skilled at covering their tracks."

Chapter 3

"One Million Pounds for Missing Princess!" screamed the front page of Sunday's *London Journal*. Elizabeth and Luke saw the headline at a crowded newsstand in London, after they left Victoria Station that morning.

"Pembroke is at it again," Luke complained. He shoved through the crowd to pick up a copy of the newspaper, reaching past a teenage couple with stiff green hair and a middle-aged man walking a poodle. The dog began yelping loudly at Luke, straining at its leash.

"You'd better watch it, chap," the green-haired boy said, laughing at him. "That little yapper is out for your blood!"

Elizabeth shuddered at the word "blood," but Luke just cast the youth a dirty look and threw a few coins on the counter. Elizabeth could hear the sound of the poodle's frantic barking following them as she and Luke began walking along Victoria Street.

The train station had a connection to the tube, but Elizabeth and Luke had chosen to walk.

"It's hard to believe that a newspaper with the *Journal's* sterling reputation would sensationalize this missing princess bit all over the front page, day after day," Luke said, handing her the newspaper. "You read it. I can't bear to."

"I thought Pembroke sunk to a new low yesterday," Elizabeth said, "with that fantasy about the Tokyo bathhouse. Next it'll be 'Missing Princess Abducted by Space Aliens.'"

She scanned the article. "At least today's story is true. The paper is putting up a huge reward for information leading to the return of Princess Eliana."

"It's just another excuse for Pembroke to cover up the really big story," Luke scoffed. "This front-page headline should be about Joy Singleton's murder."

"But why is he doing this?" Elizabeth asked. "He knows there's a murderer on the loose. Why would he endanger a whole city?"

"He's protecting somebody," Luke said. "And that's not surprising, with the suspect list narrowed down to just Pembroke, his wife, and Robert."

"We still can't prove that," Elizabeth reminded him.

"We will," Luke said, staring with interest at the article. "Actually, Pembroke may have done us a big favor with today's edition. A million pounds just might induce someone to turn in the missing princess." He rolled his eyes. "Unless, of course, she really has been kidnapped, or is in Japan, or has been abducted by space aliens."

"And if the princess is returned home soon, safe

and sound, Pembroke will lose his smoke screen!" Elizabeth said. "He won't have an excuse to bury the murder stories at the back of the newspaper anymore."

Luke stopped walking and faced Elizabeth. "And," he said, his voice rising with excitement, "people will realize that the *Journal* made up those stories about Tokyo and kidnapping. Pembroke's cover-up will be exposed."

Elizabeth shook her head. "It's a nice theory, Luke, but nobody's going to turn Lina in. Nobody else knows who—"

She gasped, realizing what she had said.

Luke's mouth dropped open. "Lina?" he asked loudly. He glanced around guiltily and then softened his voice. "Are you saying what I think you're saying?"

"Please, Luke. I'm the only one who knows, and I promised her I wouldn't tell a soul. I never should have opened my big mouth. You won't tell anyone, will you?"

Luke pulled her to a secluded bench a few meters off the sidewalk. "Elizabeth, are you telling me that your roommate, working-class Lina from Liverpool, is really the missing Princess Eliana—the youngest daughter of the queen of England?"

Elizabeth nodded, sick that she'd divulged Eliana's secret. "She's tired of being sheltered and elite. She wanted to meet real people and see what the real London is like, so she ran away from Buckingham Palace, moved into HIS, and found a job in a soup kitchen."

Luke leaned over and kissed her. "Elizabeth Wakefield, you are just full of surprises. All you have to do now is write up an article about the princess's real whereabouts, and Pembroke's cover-up will be exposed. If Tony won't print it in the *Journal*, I'm sure an editor at some other newspaper in town would be happy to."

Elizabeth jumped up from the bench. "Luke! I can't betray Lina's confidence! Besides, exposing the cover-up wouldn't do much good right now—not until we're sure of exactly what Pembroke's covering up."

Luke sighed. "I guess you're right," he admitted. "And don't be alarmed. I won't reveal her royal highness's secret if you don't want me to. In fact, I admire the girl for what she's doing. But when we have enough evidence to go to the police, you may need to convince Lina—or Eliana—to turn herself in. After all, lives are at stake."

Elizabeth remembered the sight of Joy's body on the blood-spattered sheets of Jessica's bed. Her stomach gave a sickening lurch.

"Especially *Jessica's* life," she whispered.

"Welcome home," Eliana said to Elizabeth as the American girl walked into the dorm room at noon on Sunday. It felt good to put aside her fake Liverpudlian accent and speak instead in her natural, softer tones. Elizabeth was the only person she could truly be herself around.

Then Eliana laughed. "Home. It's strange how quickly I've come to think of this place as home."

Elizabeth glanced around the spacious but messy dorm room and raised her eyebrows.

"My mother would be horrified if she knew where

I was living," Lina continued. "Actually, I called her again this morning—from a pay phone across town, so she can't trace me. I was afraid that today's *Journal* article would upset her—a bounty on my head and all. So I called to tell her that I'm still all right, but that I can't bear the thought of going back to my old life yet. She's furious with me."

"I'm sure she's just concerned about your safety."

"That's for certain. Mum is so overprotective that it's like living with a prison warden!"

Elizabeth laughed. "With Buckingham Palace as the world's best-decorated prison."

"Did you see today's *Journal*, by the way? The going rate for a princess is now one million pounds."

"Don't worry about anyone trying to collect it," Elizabeth said reassuringly. "Your secret is safe with me." Then she looked away, blushing.

"Liz, what's wrong?"

Elizabeth sat down on the bottom bunk. "To tell you the truth, your secret isn't safe with me. I accidentally told Luke about you, just a half hour ago. I'm sorry, but it slipped out."

Eliana felt a stab of fear. "Is he going to turn me in?"

"No, of course not," Elizabeth said quickly. "You can trust Luke—and me, even though I haven't given you much reason to."

Eliana relaxed again. Elizabeth looked so miserable that she felt sorry for her. "It's all right, Liz. I know *you* trust Luke. That's good enough for me. Besides, I'm too happy today to let it bother me. And I owe it all to you."

Elizabeth looked at her expectantly, though

Eliana could see that her mind wasn't really on the conversation.

"David and I went out together last night and had a marvelous time!" Eliana bubbled. "You know, I've lived in London all my life, but I've missed so much of the city. David and I explored it together. We were real tourists—Westminster Abbey, St. Paul's Cathedral. We even dropped by Buckingham Palace to watch the changing of the guard! Of course, I wore my dark glasses for that."

Elizabeth smiled. "I'm glad you had a good time."

"It's amazing how much David and I have in common, Elizabeth. For one thing, our politics are exactly alike." She stared at her fingernails for a moment. "He'll hate me if he ever learns the truth about who I am. You know, we both despise the whole idea of royalty, the idea that some people were born to have power and wealth and position, just because they're descended from a line of interbred snobs. You have a much better system in America."

"We have problems in America, too," Elizabeth said absently.

Eliana crossed the room and sat beside her. "You sound as if you're a thousand miles away. What's the matter, Liz? Are you still upset about telling Luke my secret?"

Elizabeth shook her head. "No, Eliana. I'm fine."

Eliana clapped her hand to her mouth. "Oh, I almost forgot to tell you! Here's a bit of news to cheer you up. Rene was in here looking for you this morning. He has to attend an embassy function for most of the day, but he left you a message. He asked me to tell you he's sorry for acting, as he put it, 'like a spurned lover.' He wants to be friends now, and asked if you'll meet him for lunch tomorrow."

Elizabeth's blue-green eyes lit up. "That's wonderful, Eliana! I'll leave him a note accepting the invitation."

"Good. But you still haven't told me what's wrong, Elizabeth. Didn't you have a good time at Pembroke Manor?"

"No . . . I didn't," she said, getting up from the bunk. "Suddenly I'm starving. Will you excuse me if I go downstairs to raid the kitchen? I'll fill you in on what happened later."

Eliana watched the American girl thoughtfully as she headed out of the room. Elizabeth had seemed agitated for most of the week—ever since the night she and Eliana came across the mangled body of a Yorkshire terrier on a foggy London street. Elizabeth had recognized poor Poo-Poo as the subject of her missing dog story at the newspaper.

Eliana shivered at the memory of the Yorkie's body, the blood on its throat glistening crimson in the moonlight. She couldn't imagine what had happened at Pembroke Manor to further upset Elizabeth. But somehow, she knew it was related to Poo-Poo's bloody death.

Jessica walked into the kitchen of HIS Sunday afternoon and set her suitcase on the floor. She was surprised to see her sister at the table, reading the most recent issue of the *London Journal* and eating leftover chicken.

47

"I didn't know you were back!" Elizabeth began.

"Robert just dropped me off," Jessica explained. "I haven't even been upstairs yet. Is there any more of that fried chicken?"

"Help yourself."

Jessica poked the front page of Elizabeth's newspaper. "How about that million-dollar reward Robert's father is offering for the missing princess?" she asked. "The Pembrokes are just about the most generous people I've ever met."

"It's a million *pounds*," Liz corrected her.

Jessica rolled her eyes. "What difference does it make? A million is a million. Somebody's going to get rich by finding Eliana. Too bad it can't be us. Maybe we've been investigating the wrong news story. If you were a princess, where would you go?"

Instead of answering her question, Elizabeth changed the subject. "How was your dinner date with Robert last night?"

Jessica sighed dreamily. "You should have seen the restaurant, Liz. There were enough forks at my place setting to stock the whole silver department at Simpson's department store back home. We ate chateaubriand—that's steak, you know. And trifle—a scrumptious dessert with layers of fruit and custard and sponge cake and I don't know what else. There was candlelight and soft music and the world's best-looking waiters. It was the most elegant dinner I've ever had!"

"How nice," Elizabeth said without much enthusiasm.

"Robert is just amazing, Liz. He knows absolutely

everyone worth knowing in England. A member of parliament stopped by our table to say hello. *A member of parliament!"*

"It sounds like fun."

"Then why do you look as if you've just eaten a sour pickle?"

"Oh, don't mind me, Jessica. I'm still recovering from what happened this weekend."

"What's to recover from? It's over and done with. Of course, I feel awful about Joy. But there isn't anything we can do about it. She would want us to go on having a great time in England. And, Liz, I am having one heckuva great time! I haven't been this happy since before Sam died. I didn't think I would ever love another boy the way I loved Sam. But I do, Liz. I'm in love with Robert Pembroke. This is definitely the Big L!"

Elizabeth looked startled. "Are you sure it's Robert you're in love with, and not just the money and the celebrities and the expensive dinners?"

Jessica folded her arms impatiently. "Give me a little credit, Liz. I'm not *that* superficial. Robert is kind, generous, and a lot of fun. He really cares about me. Of course, having tons of money and being related to royalty is always a plus in a boyfriend. But you know I wouldn't date someone who was *naff*, or a real *narg*, just because he was rich."

"Naff? Narg? I had no idea you were bilingual."

"They're British words," Jessica said with an air of importance. "Robert taught them to me. Naff means uncool, and a narg is a nerd—like your friend Winston Egbert in Sweet Valley. In fact, most of your *mates* in Sweet Valley are nargs."

"*My* friend! Winston is *our* friend, and as for—"

"Oh, cool off, Liz. I'm only kidding," she lied. "The point is that I'm in love with Robert Pembroke and he's in love with me. My own twin sister should be happy for me."

"I'm happy that you're happy, Jess. But I think you're rushing into this. Isn't it awfully soon to be talking about love? I mean, you met Robert less than a week ago. There are probably a lot of things you don't know about him . . ."

Jessica jumped from her seat. "What did Robert ever do to you?" she yelled. "Why do you hate him so much?"

"I don't hate Robert. It's just that—"

"Besides, you've known Luke less than a week, too. Why is it all right for you to be serious about him, if it's not all right for me and Robert? You're only four minutes older than me, Liz. You have no right to tell me how to live my life!"

"But Jessica, I—"

"I don't have to stand here and listen to you criticize the guy I love," Jessica shouted. "I'm fed up with your bossy, holier-than-thou attitude!" She stormed out of the room.

Elizabeth pounded a fist into her open palm as she watched Jessica's retreating back. "Sometimes she makes me so mad—" she said aloud. Then she noticed Eliana hesitating in the doorway.

"I didn't mean to eavesdrop, Liz," Eliana began. "And I'll leave if you want me to. But are you all right? I was reading in the library and I couldn't help hearing—"

"It's OK," Elizabeth said. "You might as well come in. And I'm fine. I just get so angry with Jessica sometimes! I don't know why I bother trying to help her. All I get for it is yelled at. She's so absorbed in little Lord Robert that she won't pay attention to anyone else. But I don't trust Robert or his family. And what happened at Pembroke Manor this weekend certainly didn't increase my confidence. I just know they're hiding something."

"I'm still in the dark about just what happened this weekend," Eliana reminded her.

Elizabeth took a deep breath and described her discovery of Joy's body in Jessica's bed Saturday morning. "I'm not accusing Robert of being a murderer," she admitted. "At least, I don't think I am. But somebody who was in that house this weekend *is* a murderer, and the evidence seems to point to the Pembrokes."

She decided not to mention the werewolf connection just yet, realizing how crazy it would sound.

"Even aside from the murders, I don't think Robert Pembroke is the kind of guy my sister should be going out with. He has a terrible reputation, and I don't want to see her get hurt. After all, she hardly knows him, and now she's convinced that she's in love. Tell me honestly, Eliana," she concluded. "Was I out of line to caution her against jumping into this relationship so quickly?"

Eliana looked thoughtful. "No," she decided. "It's never out of line to be concerned about somebody you love. But in this case, I can tell you that you don't need to worry so much. I know Robert; in fact, the

Pembrokes are distant cousins of mine. Certainly, the family isn't everyone's cup of tea. They're much too— *aristocratic*." She smiled ironically.

"Robert's been a bit of a handful for his parents," Eliana continued, "but it's only with schoolboy pranks and that type of thing. He's not a bad sort. And I'm a hundred percent certain that he doesn't have it in him to be a killer. The worst injury Jessica could get from Robert is a broken heart, when he moves on to his next conquest."

Elizabeth sighed deeply. "I'm relieved to hear you say so, Eliana. I hope you're right. I do know that there's no real evidence for accusing him of murder."

"Of course there isn't," Eliana said. "And what possible motive would he have for murdering the young woman at Pembroke Manor?"

Elizabeth shook her head. "None that I can think of."

"Maybe you're overreacting to Jessica's relationship with Robert. It's only natural to want to protect your sister, but she's sixteen years old—old enough to make her own decisions."

"And old enough to make her own mistakes," Elizabeth pointed out. "But you're right. If Robert turns out to be a rat, Jessica will have to learn about it on her own—though I still plan to keep an eye on her."

Elizabeth fingered the newspaper on the table in front of her. "If you know Robert," she said thoughtfully, "then you know his father, as well. You, of all people, must have noticed the way the *Journal* is exploiting the missing princess story. What would

Pembroke have to gain from plastering you all over his newspaper?"

Eliana shrugged. "The coverage is annoying, but I don't question Lord Pembroke's interest in using his newspaper to help find me. As I said, we are cousins."

"All the same, it seems like there would be more important news to cover than this steady stream of princess stories. No offense."

Eliana laughed. "I suppose it must seem strange to an American, but to the British, anything dealing with the royal family—even idle gossip—*is* important news."

"Come on, Eliana. A kidnapping? A Tokyo bath-house? Both of those stories were based entirely on hearsay."

"All right, so the *Journal* has gone a bit overboard. But I'm certain the stories are selling a lot of newspapers. Why do you think there's something sinister behind them?"

"Joy's murder was not the first one of its kind. You know about Dr. Neville and Poo-Poo. There was also a nurse, about a month ago. Every time, the newspaper had the information, but buried it toward the back of the paper, or refused to run the stories altogether. Doesn't it seem odd to you that the owner of the *Journal* was at a murder scene yesterday, yet there's no mention of it in today's newspaper? He's protecting somebody, Eliana. And I intend to find out who."

"Actually, it doesn't seem odd in the least," Eliana said, "not if you know Lord Pembroke. The man has a terrific fear of scandal. For instance, he had the courtroom closed to the public the last time Robert was arrested for traffic violations. And when Robert was kicked out of his most recent school, Lord Pembroke endowed a new wing for the school's library—in exchange for having the records say Robert transferred out of his own accord."

"So you think Lord Pembroke is using the princess stories to cover up something terrible Robert has done?"

"I didn't say that!" Eliana protested. "I'm just trying to explain that Lord Pembroke doesn't want to sully the family name—for instance, by allowing a newspaper article that says a body was found at Pembroke Manor. He may not be covering up the identity of the murderer, Liz. He could be more interested in covering up the location of the murder."

"I know what it's like to have your family's name dragged through the mud," Elizabeth admitted, biting her lip. "Not long ago, I was in court myself—Jessica's boyfriend was killed in an accident, and I was driving the car. The accident turned out to be someone else's fault. But I would have given anything for a news blackout up until that point!"

Eliana looked startled. "Oh, Liz! How awful that must have been for you. I had no idea. But maybe that experience will help you understand Pembroke's actions. I remember hearing that the Pembrokes were involved in some sort of scandal fifteen or twenty years ago. Since then, Lord Pembroke has been fanatical about keeping the family name clean."

"What kind of scandal?" Elizabeth asked.

"I don't remember. It must have happened a year

or two before I was born. But as a child, I heard of a deep, dark secret that was causing the Pembrokes great embarrassment."

Very interesting, Elizabeth mused, wondering if the old scandal was somehow tied in with the current goings-on. *Now if I could only find out what the big scandal was.*

Unfortunately, the Pembrokes were the only logical source of information on the old scandal. Jessica would have a fit if Elizabeth went anywhere near Robert; besides, Robert would have been a baby at the time. The elder Lord Pembroke was already suspicious of Elizabeth. That left only Robert's mother. Elizabeth decided she would have to question Lady Pembroke about the twenty-year-old scandal—and about the recent murders.

I'll get to the bottom of this mystery if it's the last thing I do!

Chapter 4

"What with Lucy gone and all, this is going to be a crazy week for me," Tony Frank told the twins early Monday morning. "And I'm sorry to say that supervising interns isn't terribly high on the priority list. You'll have some assignments, but I'm afraid you'll be on your own a lot, too. So plan to do a lot of sightseeing, or whatever it is that American teenagers do in London."

Jessica grinned, thinking this way she'd finally have time to hit the stores. *Will it be Harrods or Bond Street?*

Elizabeth, though, had a thoughtful look on her face.

"Tony," Elizabeth began, "you don't mind if I spend some of that extra time tracking down some stories on my own, do you?"

Jessica rolled her eyes. It was just like her narg of a sister to want to spend the week writing. Well, she was still mad at Elizabeth for criticizing Robert, and she wasn't going to waste a moment worrying about whether Elizabeth was having fun this week.

"Still thinking about that Pulitzer, Liz?" Tony replied. "Go right ahead. I like reporters who take the initiative. Just don't get in over your head. Leave the breaking news to the professionals. Well, I guess that's singular now," he said, referring to Lucy's absence.

"Do you think Lucy is gone for good, Tony?" Elizabeth asked, taking his cue.

"I'm afraid so, Elizabeth," Tony answered. "And I'm also afraid you're looking at the *London Journal*'s new crime desk editor."

"Congratulations!" Jessica said, happy for Tony's success but sorry that it meant she wouldn't be seeing any more of the grouchy but glamorous Friday. "That's more exciting than covering tea parties for the society desk."

"I've wanted this job all my life," Tony admitted. "Though I hate the idea that I'm here only because Lucy resigned."

"And I guess this isn't going to make her any more likely to want to make up with you," Jessica said sympathetically.

Tony's face fell. Jessica had known from the start that Tony was in love with Lucy, even though they spent most of their time together bickering, arguing, and just plain yelling at each other. Lucy had accused Tony of sensationalizing the princess story in order to get the crime desk job for himself. Now that Tony had the position, Jessica reflected, their chances for a reconciliation were zilch.

"It's too bad about Lucy," Elizabeth said. "She seemed difficult to get to know, but she's a first-rate journalist."

"You're right on both counts," Tony agreed. "I'm the first to admit that Lucy's really the best *man* for the crime desk job. It'll be tough to fill her court shoes."

Jessica stared at him. "Huh?"

"You know, *court* shoes." Tony laughed. "High-heeled pumps, in American."

Jessica sighed. "Why can't the English speak English, like regular people?"

"Because regular people are naffs and nargs," Elizabeth said, reminding Jessica that she'd been dropping a few Briticisms herself.

"Speaking of words," Tony said, laughing, "I've got an assignment I want you both to work on this morning." Jessica's visions of shopping dimmed. "In the last week you two have been assigned a number of disparate topics—everything but the kitchen sink, in fact. Today, we'll remedy that deficiency."

"That sounds ominous," Elizabeth said.

"We're calling this the Case of the Flying Sink," Tony continued. "It seems that a university student was walking down Tottenham Court Road, when he was hit on the head by a kitchen sink that came soaring through the air."

The twins groaned in unison. "Another Bumpo story!" they exclaimed. Sergeant Bumpo was the bungling Scotland Yard detective who always handled the most ridiculous cases.

I'd rather be shopping, Jessica thought ruefully.

59

"Well, I guess we'd better catch up with Bumpo," Elizabeth said with a sigh after Tony dismissed the twins. Jessica knew that Elizabeth was itching to show off her journalistic skills on the Case of the Werewolf Murders. *How could calm, reasonable Elizabeth have turned into such a basket case that she actually believes in werewolves?*

Jessica glanced up and saw the answer to her question: Luke. He had somehow convinced Elizabeth that a werewolf could be responsible for the deaths of Joy and the other victims.

Luke smiled warmly at Elizabeth. "Would you like to go to the cinema with me tonight, Liz? *The Howling* is playing at the Paradiso."

"That would be great," Elizabeth replied, smiling and actually sounding pleased at an invitation to watch a werewolf movie.

Jessica shook her head. The old Elizabeth thought horror movies were childish. Then Jessica remembered a snatch of an old Warren Zevon song and began singing tunelessly: "'Ow-ooooh! Werewolves of London! Ow-ooooh!'"

"Jessica!" Elizabeth protested.

Jessica folded her arms in front of her. "I can't believe this. You two are taking this goofy werewolf stuff too seriously."

"Don't make light of werewolves, Jessica," Luke said in a quiet voice. "They're very serious business."

Luke leaned over to kiss Elizabeth on the forehead. "I'll come by your dorm at eight," he said, then crossed the room and disappeared through the door, leaving Jessica shaking her head in disgust.

60

"So, Sergeant Bumpo, have you determined where the flying sink came from?" Elizabeth asked the short, round detective, trying to keep the impatience out of her voice.

"Certainly. It was dropped from the window of the sixth-floor flat."

Jessica grimaced. "Why would anyone try to kill a college student by dropping a kitchen sink on his head?"

"I have conducted an intensive investigation on that very point," Bumpo said in an important-sounding voice. "Fingerprints, interviews with witnesses, analysis of the forensic evidence—"

"And what did you discover?" Elizabeth interrupted. Bumpo loved using every investigative technique known to criminal science—and he loved talking about them even more. Usually, Elizabeth found him amusing, but today she was in a hurry to go question Lady Pembroke—if she could find an excuse to get away from Jessica.

"After serious examination of the evidence," Bumpo said, "I've determined that the young fellow was hit entirely by accident. It seems a carpenter in the sixth-floor flat was installing a new washbasin. The old one was rather heavy to tote down the stairs, and the lift wasn't working, so he dropped it out the window instead. Unfortunately, he failed to notice the poor chap walking past, below."

"So what's the condition of the, uh, victim?" Elizabeth asked.

"The fellow's doing splendidly—conscious and in

61

good spirits," the detective replied. "He's in hospital, of course, but it's only a slight concussion. Luckily, he's a jolly strapping youth—university football player, you know."

Jessica brightened. "Football player?"

Bumpo wiped a hand across the top of his head, as if to assure himself that his few wisps of hair still shielded his rather large bald spot. "I suppose that's *soccer* to you Americans, isn't it?"

Suddenly, Elizabeth knew how to get away from her sister. In love or not, Jessica never passed up a chance to meet a good-looking college boy.

"Jessica," Elizabeth said, "I think it's very important that we interview the victim. Would you mind heading over to the hospital to question him? I'll stay here and finish up with Sergeant Bumpo. Then I'm meeting Rene for lunch. I'll see you at the *Journal* later this afternoon, and we'll write up the story."

Jessica smiled gratefully, ignoring the fact that she was angry with Elizabeth. "I think you're absolutely right," she said. "I'll get over to the hospital right away."

After Jessica was gone, Elizabeth hurried through the rest of her discussion with Sergeant Bumpo and then took a taxi to the Pembrokes' fashionable Eaton Square home, Pembroke Green.

Ciao for now to the Case of the Flying Sink, she thought as she sank back into the cushy seat of the distinctive black Austin, London's standard taxi. As exciting as it was to work for a real, big-city newspaper, Elizabeth had been bitterly disappointed by the types of articles she was assigned to write. She knew it was unrealistic to expect to cover a major story—she *was* just a high-school intern. But she was sure she could do it. Maybe her private investigation of the werewolf murders would give her the chance.

As London flew past her window, Elizabeth imagined her byline on a page-one *Journal* exclusive, "Murder Suspect Apprehended."

She smiled at the familiar daydream. Then she gave a long sigh and forced herself to concentrate on her upcoming interview with Lady Pembroke.

"What do the Pembrokes have to hide?" she asked under her breath. Lady Pembroke might not know about the *Journal*'s cover-up of the murders, but she would certainly remember the scandal that had rocked the family name fifteen or twenty years earlier.

Whether she would tell Elizabeth—or rather, Jessica—was another question entirely. Unclasping her hair from its neat ponytail and stuffing the barrette into her purse, Elizabeth began her transformation into Jessica, who usually wore her hair down. Then she pulled out a lipstick and applied it liberally; Elizabeth seldom wore makeup, but Jessica wouldn't think of walking into the Pembrokes' town house without it.

A few minutes later, "Jessica" sat in a sumptuously furnished parlor with Lady Pembroke. A butler hovered nearby, waiting to refill their teacups—and glaring suspiciously at Elizabeth.

Why didn't I put more thought into my clothes today? she silently chastised herself, looking down at her simple navy skirt and white blouse. Lady

Pembroke, of course, was dressed impeccably, in a cream-colored silk suit and a strand of pearls. Not surprising, considering this was a woman who owned at least one mink coat that was worth roughly as much as a four-year college education in the States.

"Thanks for seeing me on the spur of the moment like this, Lady Pembroke," she said with exactly the right amount of Jessica's bounce in her voice. "I was in the neighborhood, and had just a few questions to go over with you, about your missing mink coat."

Lady Pembroke looked down her long, thin nose. "I thought we had exhausted the topic when you and that dreadful Sergeant Bumpo interviewed me last week," she said. "But go ahead, if you must. Especially if it will help recover my mink."

"As I understand it," Elizabeth said carefully, "you checked your mink while you were having tea at Browns. When you went to claim it afterward, you were given a chinchilla instead."

"A simply *wretched* chinchilla," Lady Pembroke emphasized.

Elizabeth stifled an urge to roll her eyes. Instead, she pretended to write in her reporter's notebook. "I suppose you were having tea with your husband, Lord Pembroke?"

"No, I was not," Lady Pembroke replied, narrowing her eyes.

"Then you were alone."

"Miss Wakefield, a woman of breeding never dines alone in public. I was with friends, of course—as I said in my statement to the detective. But I fail to see what difference it makes who my companions were."

64

Elizabeth smiled, hoping she looked friendlier than she felt. "I was just wondering if there were any other witnesses to the, uh, crime. But you're right; I can get that information from Sergeant Bumpo's report. So I won't waste any more of your time on it."

Lady Pembroke sniffed. "See that you don't. But I am gratified that somebody at the newspaper is taking this case seriously. My husband certainly isn't. And that horrible little Scotland Yard detective seemed to think the disappearance of my mink was a simple misunderstanding. I, for one, am convinced that a crime has taken place."

"I'm sure you're right, Lady Pembroke," Elizabeth agreed. Then she decided to press her advantage. "You know, a thorough newspaper article has a way of bringing a crime like this out into the open. The more information I have, the easier it will be for the police to recover your mink. For instance, does anyone have a reason to hold a grudge against you or your family? Even an incident that took place a very long time ago—like twenty years ago—could cause somebody to perpetrate a crime like this, for revenge."

Lady Pembroke's perfectly manicured fingers gripped her teacup tighter, her long, pink fingernails clinking against the fine bone china. When she stood up, her eyes were flashing, and Elizabeth realized she had gone too far.

"I have no idea what you are alluding to," Lady Pembroke said in a furious but perfectly controlled voice. "I understand that my son thinks quite highly of you, but I find you to be a boorish, ill-bred young woman. This interview is over."

"So this is the newsroom," Emily said, coming up behind Jessica, who sat at a computer on Monday afternoon, typing the day's Bumpo article with two fingers. "Are you ready to go out for tea?"

Jessica grimaced. "Not until I finish this stupid story for the evening edition."

"Another exploding aubergine? Or was it a turnip this time?"

"Ha, ha. Very funny," Jessica said. "But this happens to be an important article. A college student was injured in a major accident this morning. It was, uh, water-related."

"Oh, really? A boating accident? That does sound important. Let me see—"

Jessica tried to block Emily's view of the computer screen, but she was too slow.

Emily burst out laughing. "A kitchen sink fell on his head? I've heard of it raining cats and dogs, but never plumbing fixtures!"

Jessica laughed in spite of herself. "What a waste of a perfectly good morning. The guy who got clobbered by it wasn't even good-looking—tons of acne, and no neck!"

"Speaking of good-looking, wasn't Elizabeth having lunch with Rene today? How did that go?"

Jessica raised her eyebrows. "Apparently, it's going well. My deadbeat sister hasn't come back. That's why I'm stuck writing this story."

"Elizabeth hasn't returned? Do you suppose she finally gave in and decided that she loves Rene, after all?"

"A few weeks ago, I'd have said you were crazy.

But Elizabeth has really gone off the deep end since she's been here." She shook her head. "Nobody back home would believe it if they heard *I* was sitting in a stuffy newspaper office, writing an article that Elizabeth promised to do, while *she's* out with a great-looking French guy. It's as if she's turned into *me!*"

"What's so unusual about Elizabeth having a date?" Emily asked. "I thought she had a rather handsome boyfriend at home."

"That's just the point. She's usually boringly loyal to Todd. If she can forget all about him to have a fling with Luke, maybe she'd go out with Rene, too! I never thought I'd say this about my sister, but I've got to hand it to her—juggling three boys at once! As I said, she's sounding more and more like *me.*"

"Are you still mad at her for what she said yesterday?"

"I guess I'll get over it," Jessica said. "I wish she'd give Robert a chance. But she really thinks she's looking out for me. Liz can be kind of a mother hen. She's four minutes older than I am, and she thinks that gives her the right to boss me around!"

The phone rang. Jessica picked it up to hear Robert's voice, inviting her to dinner at Pembroke Green that night with him and his mother.

"My father won't be present, of course," Robert told her. "He's still at the manor house, taking care of some business. But I was hoping to bring you and Mother together to help you two become *reacquainted*. From what Mother said, I take it your interview with her at the house today was less than successful."

"Interview? What interview?"

"You know, the one this morning about her missing mink coat. She told me you came by to follow up on it for your newspaper story."

Jessica's eyes widened as realization swept over her. *Elizabeth went to Pembroke Green today, disguised as me!* Jessica's forgiveness faded, replaced by rage. "Oh," she said in a quiet, strained voice. "That interview."

"She seems rather upset with you, in fact," Robert continued. "I'm sure it was all a misunderstanding. She said you were asking a lot of personal questions, but I know you were just doing your job. Don't worry too much about it, Jessica. Mother can be rather difficult to get along with. But I'd like to give the two of you a chance to become friends. How about if I pick you up around six o'clock?"

"That would be fine, Robert." Jessica hung up the phone and sat quietly, her hand still clenching the receiver.

"What is it, Jess?" Emily asked. "You look upset."

"She's done it now," Jessica said in a barely controlled voice. "She's convinced that Robert's no good. She'll go to any lengths to find dirt on him. But this time, she's gone too far. And she's going to pay for it."

"Jessica, who are you talking about?" Emily asked. "What happened?"

"I think I'm finally going to have a major story to report on for the *Journal*," Jessica announced. "American Teenager Murders Twin Sister."

"My visit to Pembroke Green was disastrous,"

Elizabeth confided to Rene as they strolled through Regent's Park after lunch Monday. "Lady Pembroke practically had me thrown out of the house. I'm sure she hates me."

"Except that she thinks it is Jessica she hates," the French boy supplied.

"That's right. And Jessica will be furious when she finds out."

Rene chuckled. "Can you blame her?"

"On one hand, I hope I didn't wreck Jessica's relationship with Robert's family. But on the other hand, anything that pushes Jessica away from the Pembrokes can't be all that bad. I'm still convinced that there's something sinister going on with that family."

"Did you learn anything else of importance from Lady Pembroke?"

"Not really," Elizabeth said. "Except that she practically sneers every time she mentions her husband's name. There's no love lost between those two! You know, I didn't notice it over the weekend, but now that I think about it, they hardly said a word to each other the whole time I was at Pembroke Manor."

"A loveless marriage? Could that—how do you say, *shed some light* on the other avenues you are investigating?"

"I don't know. I keep wondering about the big scandal. Apparently something awful happened nearly twenty years ago that caused the Pembroke name to be dragged through the mud. Maybe whatever it was turned Lord and Lady Pembroke against each other. Of course," she admitted, "that's pure speculation."

"Perhaps Jessica has heard something about this scandal, in the time she has spent with the Pembrokes."

Elizabeth shook her head. "I doubt they would bring up a topic that apparently caused them so much embarrassment. And I'm certainly not going to mention it to her. She wouldn't believe anything bad about the Pembrokes anyway. She thinks they're perfect. Whatever Jessica says, I believe that Lord Pembroke knows more than he's saying about the murders of Joy Singleton and Cameron Neville. It's possible that he's the murderer himself—or that Robert or Lady Pembroke is."

"From what you've said of the lady, it sounds as if she could freeze her victims to death with a single glance. But seriously, Elizabeth, I am worried about you. This investigation is beginning to sound dangerous."

Elizabeth was touched by his concern, but she thought it was unwarranted. "Don't worry about me, Rene. I'm perfectly safe."

"Elizabeth, you have seen two mutilated bodies—three, if you include the small terrier. You've been warned to cease your inquiries into the deaths, by a man whom you admit could be the murderer—a wealthy, powerful man who's accustomed to having his every wish obeyed. How can you say you are in no danger?"

"Rene, I was at Pembroke Manor Saturday night, too. But it was Jessica's room the murderer chose, and Joy who was killed. Nobody has threatened my safety. I don't think—"

She stopped when she noticed Rene looking at her curiously.

"What's that silver pendant you're clutching so tightly, Liz?" he asked. "On the chain around your neck?"

Elizabeth blushed and let go of the necklace. "It's, um, a pentagram."

"A pentagram? Isn't that a talisman for use against werewolves?" He inspected the pendant. "Elizabeth, where did you get this?"

Elizabeth sighed. "From Luke," she said, watching Rene's face.

Rene grimaced. "Not Luke again."

"Please, Rene. Don't be upset."

Rene forced a smile. "I am trying not to be," he said. "But this is an odd gift from a beau, is it not?"

Elizabeth took a deep breath and looked him straight in the eye. "I wasn't going to tell you, Rene, because it sounds so crazy. But Luke and I believe the murderer could be a werewolf."

"Now you are jesting with me."

"No, I'm not. Look at the evidence, Rene. The bodies were found with their throats ripped out! That doesn't sound like your normal, everyday serial killer. And I found some animal fur at the scene of Joy's murder."

"Even if werewolves did exist, I thought they hunted only when the moon was full," Rene objected.

"That's not true," Elizabeth said. "Luke has been studying werewolves for years. He says they can change their shape any time they want to—though they're at their greatest strength under the full moon."

Rene just shook his head.

Elizabeth blushed again, realizing how farfetched

the theory sounded. "I see what you mean," she said haltingly. "Our evidence is pretty sketchy. And from your perspective, the idea must sound irrational."

"Completely," Rene said. "Certainly, the murders were grisly, but humans have been known to kill in horrible ways. And the animal hair could have come from a family pet—or perhaps from one of Lady Pembroke's furs."

Elizabeth sighed, knowing that Rene was right. Luke, with his love of romantic horror fiction and his lifelong interest in werewolf lore, had *wanted* the murderer to be a werewolf, so he had convinced himself that it was true. And Elizabeth, caught up in the excitement of falling in love and of having a real mystery to solve, had gone right along with him.

She glanced at Rene, walking beside her. He was practical, reasonable, and totally objective—so different from romantic, sensitive Luke. She was in love with Luke, but she resolved to be more like Rene. She would never find out what the Pembrokes were hiding if she kept allowing herself to be carried away by fantasies.

"Okay," she admitted. "There are no werewolves."

And for the first time in days, she truly believed it.

Chapter 5

Jessica was standing with her back to the door when Elizabeth walked into the girls' room at IIIS Monday evening.

"Do you think this dress makes me look fat?" Jessica chirped, modeling an elegant white sheath for Lina and Portia. Of course, Elizabeth knew, Jessica realized the dress looked stunning on her.

Jessica turned, posing for her friends. Then she caught sight of Elizabeth in the doorway, and her expression turned to poison.

"The dress looks terrific," Elizabeth said, ignoring the thunderclouds in Jessica's eyes. "And that gold jewelry is perfect with it. Are you going somewhere special tonight?"

"When I want your opinion, I'll ask for it," Jessica said acidly. "But don't hold your breath."

Lina and Portia glanced hesitantly from twin to twin, looked at each other, and silently left the room.

Elizabeth took a deep breath. "Jessica, I—"

"How could you do such a thing?" Jessica stormed. "I can't believe you would pretend to be me, just so you could spy on my boyfriend and turn his mother against me."

"It wasn't like that, Jessica, I swear! I wasn't trying to turn Lady Pembroke against you. I just needed some information—"

"Right. And now you're going to tell me it was all in the name of journalistic integrity. Darn you, Liz! You've hated my relationship with Robert from the start—you just want me to break up with him. What's the problem? Are you jealous that I'm dating a nobleman and you're not? Stringing along three guys isn't enough for you, is that it? Now you want Robert, too!"

Elizabeth was mortified that Jessica could have mistaken her motives so badly. "Jessica, you know that's not true—"

"Don't tell me what I know! One thing's for sure—I don't know *you* anymore. The sister I know wouldn't pretend to be me and bother my boyfriend's mother with a lot of rude questions! What gives you the right to pry into Robert's life?"

"Jessica, you've got to believe me. I'm not investigating Robert. This has nothing to do with your relationship with him. A killer is on the loose! My investigation of why Lord Pembroke is covering up the murder stories in the newspaper may lead to the murderer!"

Jessica's voice was laden with sarcasm. "Oh, I remember. That's the same investigation where you discovered a ferocious werewolf, stalking the streets of London, hunting its next victim! England will certainly sleep easier tonight, knowing you and Luke the kook are on the job! Face it, Liz—you two are out of control. Covering murders is way out of your league. Maybe you should stick to homicidal kitchen sinks."

"Jessica," Elizabeth said, trying to keep her voice even, "I'm sorry I upset Robert's mother. But the Pembrokes are hiding something important about the murders."

"The Pembrokes have nothing to do with the deaths, and you don't have a shred of evidence that proves otherwise! Well, I'm not going to take the rap for your obnoxious questions. How do you think Lady Pembroke will respond when she hears who really interviewed her this morning?"

Elizabeth grabbed Jessica by the shoulders and stared at her wildly. "Please, Jessica," she said, aghast. "You absolutely cannot tell the Pembrokes the truth about the interview today. If you do, you'll tip off Lord Pembroke that I'm investigating him, and you'll blow any chance I have of discovering who the murderer is!"

To Elizabeth's surprise, her sister burst into tears. "You've ruined everything!" she screamed. "I love Robert! I wanted so badly to fit in with his family, but now his mother hates me! The worst part about it is that I can't even tell her it was you at Pembroke Green today. If I do, she'll think I come from a family of complete flakes! Why couldn't you mind your own business for a change? I never want to speak to you again!"

Jessica ran out of the room, slamming the door behind her. Elizabeth sighed. But she couldn't spend time worrying about Jessica's anger. The important thing right now was to find the murderer, even if it meant rattling any skeletons that hid in the Pembroke closet.

It wasn't me! Jessica wanted to scream at dinner Monday night. *I didn't ask you all those obnoxious questions! It was my evil twin, Elizabeth!*

Instead, she took another bite of the perfectly prepared pheasant, and wished she could savor the sumptuous meal. Unfortunately, under Lady Pembroke's icy glare everything she ate tasted like sawdust.

"So, Jessica," Lady Pembroke began in a cold, hard voice. "Are you enjoying your work as a reporter? Your interview style is rather—unsubtle. I had heard that Americans prize directness. In England we favor a more moderate approach."

"Please, Mother," Robert interjected. "It's a reporter's business to ask a lot of questions."

Jessica smiled gratefully at him, but Lady Pembroke raised her eyebrows, obviously unimpressed.

It's hard to defend myself when I don't know what I'm defending, Jessica thought. Unfortunately, she still wasn't sure exactly what Elizabeth had asked that morning. Maybe she could get Lady Pembroke to tell her.

"I am so sorry if some of my questions were too personal," Jessica said, hating herself for taking the blame for Elizabeth's blundering. "But I'm still very new at this reporting thing, and I was feeling nervous, interviewing someone of your, uh, stature. Maybe you could help me improve my skills. Can you tell me just which questions were, um, inappropriate?"

Lady Pembroke sniffed, as if the unfortunate questions had left an odor that still wafted through the halls of Pembroke Green. "*All* of your questions were inappropriate, young lady."

"Mother—" Robert protested.

"In particular," Lady Pembroke amended quickly, with a glance in Robert's direction, "the question about Pembroke family history was in exceedingly poor taste. And the identity of my dining companion was entirely irrelevant to my stolen mink."

Jessica was mystified. *Family history? Dining companion?* She couldn't believe her sister had seen fit to conduct a background check on one of the oldest, most respected families in England—all because she was afraid Robert wasn't good enough to date Jessica. Who did Elizabeth think she was? The Pembrokes were related to the royal family! What would Elizabeth look for next—character references?

Robert took Jessica's hand and his mother's, and squeezed them both heartily. "It's marvelous that you two have managed to clear the air so quickly, and can now go on to become friends," he said hopefully.

Lady Pembroke made a noise that sounded like "Humph."

She hates me, Jessica told herself. *Elizabeth has destroyed my chances of ever fitting in with Robert's family.*

"I apologize for my mother," Robert said later, as

he escorted Jessica outside to his silver Jaguar convertible for the drive back to HIS. "But don't worry. In time, she'll come to love you as much as I do."

"I wouldn't bet on it," Jessica said glumly. "Eliz— I mean, *I've* made her so mad that she'll never forgive me."

"That isn't true," Robert insisted, gently brushing a stray lock of golden hair out of her eyes. "But even if it were, it wouldn't matter. I don't need my mother's permission to be in love with you."

Robert was definitely the most wonderful boy in the whole world.

"You said Tony Frank wants you to adopt a relaxed attitude toward the *Journal* this week," he said. "Why don't you take Wednesday off and spend it with me? We'll take the Jag and go for a drive in the country—with the top down if the weather holds. Have you been to Stonehenge yet?"

Jessica raised her eyebrows. "Isn't it just a bunch of old rocks?"

"Oh, no," Robert explained, staring intently into her eyes. "It's much more than that. It's you and me, Jessica—all alone in the countryside—with nothing around us but lonely fields and the open road."

Robert's hands slid to Jessica's back. When his full, warm lips met hers, she felt tremors radiating through her whole body.

After they kissed, Robert held her at arm's length. "So, do we have a date?" he asked. "Do you want to go to Stonehenge with me on Wednesday?"

Jessica smiled dreamily. "I'm *dying* to."

❖   ❖   ❖

"Humans are our prey," said a gnarled, unshaven man. The werewolves, all in human form, were slowly circling Karen White, the television reporter.

A raven-haired woman panted at the reporter, her face twisted into a hungry, toothy leer. "She's ours now."

Elizabeth jumped as something hairy touched her arm. Then she realized it was only the sheepskin cuff of Luke's jacket, as he reached for a handful of popcorn. Normally, horror movies left Elizabeth unaffected—she would be too busy analyzing the plot deficiencies to be terrified by the special effects. But that Monday night at the Paradiso, *The Howling* didn't seem so farfetched.

Karen had been sent to a colony in the woods to recover from an attack by a serial killer. But the other patients there were werewolves, and their plan was to infiltrate society.

For an instant, Elizabeth had a mental image of Pembroke Manor as the colony.

Robert Pembroke glided toward her, his fangs dripping with blood. . . . But it wasn't Elizabeth he was approaching; the blondes had switched beds. It was Jessica, and she smiled serenely and offered him her throat. . . .

Elizabeth shook her head to clear the daydream and tried to concentrate instead on the more ridiculous elements of the film's plot. *This is a stupid movie,* she told herself. *There's no such thing as werewolves.* But other images kept crowding into her brain.

She saw Dr. Neville's body lying on floral carpeting in a pool of blood, murdered *as if by a wild beast*. She saw the jewels sparkling in the moonlight from Poo-Poo's crimson-stained dog collar. She saw Luke, bending over a low shrub covered with hooded flowers—wolfsbane, he'd said, which blooms only when the werewolf is stalking its prey. She thought of the Pembrokes' sheep, mutilated. Then Elizabeth remembered the scrap of fur, caught in the door frame, and the full moon streaming through the casement window of Joy's bedroom at Pembroke Manor. *Beware the full moon.*

Last, Elizabeth saw Joy's body, lying still and cold, as the blood from the gash in her throat dripped slowly into a puddle on the floor beneath the bed.

The bed that was supposed to have been Jessica's.

"We should never try to deny the beast, the animal in us," the doctor in *The Howling* had advised.

We all have an animal side, Luke had said.

Karen White had an animal side. She returned from the colony. But she had been bitten and so was destined to become an animal herself. Elizabeth watched, mesmerized, while Karen transformed into a wolf while anchoring the evening news.

The reporter's body began to tremble. "Now, I'm going to show you something to make you believe," she said to the camera. She rose painfully from her seat and arched her neck, her eyes gleaming with an eerie light. Her anguished cry turned into a howl as hair began to transform her face and neck. Her teeth elongated into fangs, but a very human tear spilled from the corner of one eye.

By the time Karen's friend shot her, mercifully, with a silver bullet in the heart, Elizabeth's doubts about werewolves were also laid to rest. She clutched her pentagram pendant as if it were a security blanket.

"Werewolves do exist," she whispered under her breath. "And one of them is stalking its prey in London."

Chapter 6

"The Slaughtered Lamb," Elizabeth said, looking across her coffee cup at Luke as they sat in a pub after the movie Monday night. "Last week, I thought it was a quaint name for a pub." She shuddered. "Now I'm not so sure—after what happened Saturday night to the sheep at Pembroke Manor."

Luke shook his head sadly. "We can't dwell on that, Elizabeth. We must concentrate on proving that the Pembrokes are guilty."

"But guilty of *what*?" Elizabeth asked. "We still don't know who the murderer is—all we know for sure is that Lord Pembroke is hiding something."

"He's hiding the fact that one of the Pembrokes is a murderer," Luke said, "and a werewolf."

Elizabeth gripped the pentagram pendant that hung around her neck. "You've finally convinced me about the murderer being a werewolf. There isn't any other explanation that fits the evidence we've found.

But we can't prove that one of the Pembrokes is the murderer."

"Then we must get the proof," Luke said quietly. "And we must do it quickly. Lord Pembroke is already suspicious."

Elizabeth nodded. "He's the key to all of this. But, Luke, he hates me. He'll never agree to an interview."

"Maybe not with you," Luke said. "But he seems to be rather fond of your sister."

A smile spread across Elizabeth's face. "Yes, he is; isn't he?"

"The only catch is that Pembroke is still out at Pembroke Manor, in the country," Luke reminded her. "You'll have to come up with an excuse for going there."

Elizabeth shrugged. "The mink-coat story worked for getting into Pembroke Green today. I'll tell him I have a few more questions about the incident, for a follow-up article."

"That may sound a little *lame*—as you Americans say," Luke said. "A restaurant coat checker swapping a chinchilla for a mink is not exactly the fall of the Berlin Wall. He might not believe you're writing another article on it. Do you think you can pull it off?"

"I'm sure *I* couldn't," Elizabeth said. "But Jessica can. I'll pour on the Jessica-charm that's broken the hearts of a hundred teenage boys. He'll talk."

Late that night, Eliana leaned back into a comfortable old leather chair in the library at HIS, and smiled at Elizabeth. "Mrs. Bates looked a bit disappointed when David and I squeaked through the

84

door at the same time as you—about two seconds before curfew!"

Elizabeth laughed. "I suppose our dorm mother was looking forward to locking the three of us out of the house for the night, as soon as the clock struck eleven. She certainly loves throwing the rule book at people!"

"She'll still have a chance to exercise her pitching arm tonight," Eliana said, checking her watch. "It's now eleven thirty—a half hour past curfew. And your twin is still out with Robert. Aren't they a little late, for just having dinner at his house?"

"Maybe Robert took her somewhere afterward—probably to make up for his mother curdling the food with those wicked stares of hers. You know, Eliana, I'm sure I've ruined Jessica's chances with Robert's mother. I did a rotten job of interviewing her this morning. But it's not all my fault. Lady Pembroke seems like a totally disagreeable person."

Eliana wrinkled her nose. "She would not be my first choice for a dinner companion," she admitted. "But I wonder if Mrs. Bates will make good on her threat to lock Jessica out for being late."

"No way," Elizabeth said, shaking her head. "You know her weakness for the upper class. She's always willing to look the other way—if Jessica is out with Little Lord Pembroke. Not like you and me, who are dating commoners!"

Eliana laughed. "The only thing I'm looking forward to about ending my charade is the look on Mrs. Bates's face when she discovers the truth—that working-class Lina from Liverpool is really Princess Eliana, the queen's daughter, from Buckingham Palace!"

"What about when David finds out the truth?"

Eliana looked at the floor. "I don't even want to think about it," she said evenly, squashing down the feeling of panic that rose within her every time she thought about it. "Things are going so well for us, Elizabeth. I've never had a beau like David. Most of the boys I date are more interested in having people see us together than in getting to know me."

"How terrible," Elizabeth said. "I never thought about it that way. Of course, appearances aren't important to David."

"No, they're not. David likes me for myself. And he cares about things that are really important. For instance, he has no classes tomorrow, so he's coming with me to work, to help out in the soup kitchen."

"That's wonderful," Elizabeth said. "You both deserve to be happy."

"So do you, Liz. But you seem so preoccupied lately. I suppose it's all this business with the murders. You don't still believe Robert or someone in his family is a killer, do you?"

"I don't know what to believe." Elizabeth sighed, nervously gripping a silver pendant that hung on a chain around her neck.

Eliana wondered if Elizabeth had deeper fears about the murders—fears she was keeping secret.

"I know Lord Pembroke is related to you," Elizabeth continued, "but I also know he has arranged for the police department to help him hide the truth. I suspect that Pembroke knows who the werew—uh, *murderer* is—if he's not guilty himself."

86

Eliana gasped. "Surely you don't think Lord Pembroke is a crazed killer!"

"No, somehow I don't," Elizabeth said. "He doesn't seem like the type. But I'm determined to find out for sure. I have to learn the true identity of the murderer. Will you help me?"

Eliana squirmed uncomfortably. "I don't know, Elizabeth. As I said, the Pembrokes are my cousins—"

"Oh, I'm not asking you to dig up any dirt on them," Elizabeth assured her. "I plan to travel to Pembroke Manor tomorrow, disguised as Jessica, to see if I can get some information about the newspaper cover-up. I want to know what Pembroke is hiding under all those stories. I guess you saw the latest fantasy, in today's paper—'Did Missing Princess Elope with Palace Guard?'"

Eliana burst into laughter, but quickly stopped when she saw the frown on Elizabeth's face. "But, Liz, what if Lord Pembroke mentions to Robert that 'Jessica' came to see him, and Robert mentions it to Jess?"

Elizabeth shrugged. "It's worth the risk. When I find absolute proof that something is criminally wrong at Pembroke Manor, Jessica will have to forgive me. And I intend to find proof."

"So what do you need from me?"

"An alibi," Elizabeth said. "I'll tell Pembroke I'm working on another article about his wife's mink. But what can I tell the people at HIS and the newspaper?"

"Make up another article to work on," Eliana suggested. "There must be something of interest to report on in the vicinity of Pembroke Manor. Then all you'll need is a last-minute excuse for staying in the country overnight. I can help you by running interference here at the dorm—especially with Mrs. Bates."

Elizabeth clapped her hands together. "Ostriches!"

"As you Americans say—*come again?*"

"From the train window on my way back to London, I noticed a field with *ostriches* in it. I've heard there's quite a market for them in some parts of the world—the hide, the eggs, and even the meat. I'll ask Tony if I can interview the farmer who's raising them."

"Not bad. It's weird enough to catch an editor's interest, but minor enough so that he won't send a more senior reporter. I think you've got yourself an assignment."

Elizabeth let out a long, sad sigh.

"What's wrong?"

"Nothing. I just wish I could cover a real story— something more important than ostriches, mink coat swaps, or exploding eggplants—I mean, *aubergines.*"

"Something like 'Serial Killer Arrested'?"

"Yes," Elizabeth said with a sudden gleam in her blue-green eyes. "Something exactly like that."

A shaft of morning sunlight pushed through a crack in the heavy velvet curtains early Tuesday, intensifying the murky shadows and bright patches of light in the library of Pembroke Manor.

In the shadows in one corner of the room, the elder Lord Robert Pembroke sat at his heavy mahogany desk. He sighed heavily, absentmindedly stroking a cigarette case that gleamed silver in his hand. The grandfather clock in the parlor tolled seven sonorous times.

Pembroke exhaled loudly. "Seven o'clock in the bloody morning," he said in a slow whisper that was almost a moan. It was a full hour before his usual time for rising, but he had been awake since four, watching the light of dawn infiltrate the dark room. Usually, Pembroke slept easily—the sleep of a man who is secure in his wealthy, powerful, eminently stable existence. But that morning, he realized he had hardly slept in three days—not since Saturday's dreadful awakening, when one of the American girls had discovered the body of Thatcher's lovely fiancée.

The young lady's death was a horrible tragedy. Poor Thatcher had been a mere shell of himself since Saturday morning. Pembroke empathized completely with his friend, the chief of police; Pembroke had also lost the love of his life—a beautiful young woman with startlingly clear blue eyes and a lilting laugh. But that was long ago. He had moved on in his life, and Thatcher would, as well.

"We only have to hold out a little longer," he had told Thatcher on Saturday.

Pembroke sighed at the memory. On Saturday, he had still harbored hope.

Those hopes had begun a month earlier, at the murder scene of that unfortunate nurse back in London. By chance, Pembroke had accompanied Thatcher to lunch that day, and so was present when the chief of police inspected the murder scene.

The evidence had confused Thatcher—a gash in the throat, as if the woman had been mauled by a beast. But Pembroke understood immediately. Werewolves were his lifelong passion. He had spent hours poring over dusty volumes and faded court proceedings from medieval werewolf trials. He had recognized the signs instantly. Nurse Dolores Handley had been murdered by a werewolf.

A real werewolf! Pembroke had dreamed all his life of studying one—in person, as it were—and learning all there was to know about it.

Besides, an authentic werewolf for Pembroke's trophy collection would have been the culmination of a lifetime of exotic game hunting and the crown on his years of study of werewolf lore. It would have brought him fame and fortune—not only in his native England, but around the world. Sales of the *Journal* would skyrocket with the articles he'd print. And the name of Robert Pembroke, Sr., would be on the lips of every journalist and every enthusiast of the hunt, on every continent of the globe. It would be a far cry from the last time the Pembroke name had been the subject of major news stories, almost twenty years earlier.

Pembroke had begged Thatcher to help him suppress the evidence of the nurse's murder, to keep every fortune hunter in Europe from converging on the city. He didn't want his private werewolf hunt to escalate into a contest for amateurs.

Then came the murder of Dr. Cameron Neville. Pembroke had been deeply distressed to see the body of his oldest and dearest friend, sprawled on the carpeting of the doctor's Essex Street residence. Certainly, the torn clothing, the bits of fur scattered about the murder scene, and the telltale wound in Neville's neck had sickened Pembroke. But they had also reinforced his original theory: A werewolf was on the prowl in London. As he stood over the doctor's body, Pembroke had resolved once again to find the murderous beast. The slaying of his friend had turned his werewolf hunt into a personal mission.

At that point, he had known for sure that he would prevail in the end. Werewolves were notoriously messy about their business of killing. All Pembroke had to do was follow the clues, anticipate the beast's next actions, and watch and wait.

But it was at the scene of Neville's murder that Pembroke's fears had started. As he turned away from the body, he had noticed the silver cigarette case gleaming like moonlight on the floor.

When he recognized the distinctive silver case, Pembroke felt as if his own heart had been torn out. Finally, he had some evidence of who the werewolf could be. But the evidence pointed in a direction he did not want to investigate. Nothing could make him believe that the cigarette case's owner was a murderer—much less a werewolf.

The case could have been stolen, he had told himself. Perhaps its owner had visited Neville before the murder, despite testimony from Neville's housekeeper that the doctor had entertained no visitors.

Then, on Saturday, Joy Singleton was found dead. Pembroke still didn't believe what the cigarette case seemed to reveal about the identity of the werewolf. But he knew that others would believe it—especially after he found fragments of a fabric he recognized, stuck in the door frame of the room where the werewolf had struck. The evidence was overwhelming.

Suddenly, hiding the details of the mysterious deaths was no longer a matter of adding a new trophy to his collection. A cover-up was vital to protecting his family. The last scandal had made him the subject of derision throughout London. He had spent more than a decade rebuilding his reputation. He wasn't going to lose that reputation now.

Even more important was protecting the person who would be implicated by the evidence: the owner of the silver case.

Suddenly, a finger of shimmering sunlight jabbed through the curtains of the still-dark library. It seized the cigarette case Pembroke still turned in his hand, staining its surface a deep crimson.

Pembroke dropped the case as if it were on fire—the cigarette case that belonged to his son, Robert.

The grandfather clock in the parlor had just chimed nine o'clock when the phone rang on Pembroke's desk, startling him out of a fitful doze. Other newspaper executives insulated themselves behind armies of secretaries. Pembroke prided himself on being accessible; the *Journal*'s editors knew they could ring him up directly in his library at Pembroke Manor.

He opened his mouth to yell at editor Reeves about the latest ridiculous story concerning the Princess Eliana—*eloped with a palace guard, indeed!* Of course, Pembroke had told the editors to play up the princess story to deflect attention from the recent deaths, but the sight of that sort of fiction in his newspaper made him positively ill.

"Hello, Lord Pembroke!" exclaimed a breathless, youthful voice at the other end of the line.

For the first time in days, a genuine smile sprang to Pembroke's face. The caller could be no one but Robert's young ladyfriend, Jessica Wakefield.

"I have a few itsy-bitsy questions for you about that mink coat of Lady Pembroke's—for a follow-up article in the newspaper, of course," Jessica said brightly. "Would you mind if I dropped by Pembroke Manor this afternoon to talk to you about it?"

Pembroke chuckled to himself, flattered. The girl was charmingly transparent. The mink swap was hardly worth one newspaper article, let alone two. Obviously, the pretty young intern was paying special attention to it because it involved him. After all, along with being the owner of the newspaper she worked at, he was her beau's father. Eager to be in his good graces, she erroneously assumed that he cared about his petty wife and her blasted mink.

In addition, the girl was probably eager for an excuse to revisit Pembroke Manor. He remembered the way Jessica's eyes had gobbled up its luxurious furnishings, like the eyes of a penniless child in a sweet shop.

"I wouldn't mind at all, child," he told her. "Glad to have you anytime. In fact, you should plan to stay for supper, and to spend the night as well. We've plenty of room, and Lord knows we could use some cheer around here!"

Then his eyes narrowed as suspicions rose in his mind. "You will be alone, won't you, dear?" he asked.

"That is to say, you don't plan to bring that twin sister of yours, do you?"

"Oh, no," Jessica assured him. "I'm working on this story all by myself."

Thank goodness, he thought, as Jessica chatted on about her internship.

It was remarkable that a guileless girl like Jessica could have an identical twin who was so nosy and suspicious, Pembroke thought. Elizabeth was the Wakefield he had to watch out for. She spent entirely too much time peering into dark corners with those big blue-green eyes, and scribbling endlessly in that little notebook of hers. It was no wonder she had hooked up with young Mr. Shepherd. Pembroke's lips tightened into a thin, hard line at the thought of the boy. The young poet made him unspeakably uncomfortable. Every time he looked at Luke, he felt battered by the accusations in the boy's brilliant blue eyes. Elizabeth's choice of Luke as a companion made her doubly suspect in Pembroke's book.

"Lord Pembroke?" Jessica asked uncertainly.

"I'm sorry, dear," he said, grateful that he was speaking to charming Jessica rather than her nosy sister. "What were you saying?"

"I just asked if Lady Pembroke has said anything about me to you. I'm afraid I was a little too assertive when I interviewed her yesterday. She may be a bit upset with me."

"Don't worry yourself," he assured her. "Lady Pembroke hasn't breathed a word to me." He didn't mention the fact that he and his wife had barely spoken to each other in years—seventeen years, to be

94

exact. "And I'm sure you acted quite properly," he added. "A good reporter must be aggressive." *But don't tell your sister I said that.*

An uncharacteristic wave of sentiment swept over Pembroke, sparked by the girl's cheerful innocence and her fondness for his unfortunate son.

"Miss Wakefield—no, *Jessica*," he began. "I owe you a debt of gratitude, my dear. And a Pembroke always pays his debts."

"I don't understand."

No, of course she wouldn't. The changes she had wrought in Robert had come about naturally, just from being near her sweet influence.

"Jessica, you must realize that you're very different from other young ladies Robert has courted in the past. You wouldn't like them—a pretentious, stuffy, empty-headed lot. What I'm trying to say is that Robert has been quite a handful to discipline, at times. He's never been a bad youth, just rambunctious—untamed. But since he's been courting you, I've noticed a change. My son has more direction than he did even a short while ago. He's more responsible. And I'm certain that he's happier than he's ever been. I owe all of that to you."

The girl seemed at a loss for words.

"Jessica," Pembroke concluded soberly, "I want you to know that Robert loves you very much. Please remember that—no matter what happens."

Elizabeth paid the taxi driver and began walking up the long driveway to Pembroke manor through a misty rain.

Convincing Tony to let her cover the ostrich story had been easy. Eliana was right—ostriches were weird enough to catch his interest, but minor enough so that he didn't want to send a more senior reporter. Of course, Jessica had glowered at both of them as Tony told Elizabeth to go ahead with it. Jessica had been aching for a chance to return to Pembroke Manor; she must have realized that this story would put Elizabeth right in the neighborhood. Elizabeth felt bad about sticking her sister with today's Bumpo cases, but she knew that her investigation was more important than Jessica's jealousy.

Elizabeth sighed, thinking of what Lord Pembroke had said on the phone that morning. He had sounded so different from his usual overbearing self. He had been vulnerable—grateful, even. In other words, he had sounded like a normal, concerned father. And he thought Jessica was helping his son. For a moment, Elizabeth wondered if she and Luke were wrong about Robert and his family. But she didn't want to have sympathy for the Pembrokes; that could get in the way of her investigation.

She forced herself to remember Joy Singleton's body in Jessica's bed, and knew she had to find proof of the murderer's identity. *Even if it turns out to be the young Robert Pembroke,* she thought, remembering his father's words. Especially if it turned out to be Robert.

Elizabeth cleared the crest of the hill, and the front of stately Pembroke Manor rose into sight. Elizabeth gasped. Red lights flashed through the rain, from an ambulance that waited in front of the mansion's grand entranceway. Uniformed police officers and medical personnel rushed around the ambulance, while servants huddled together on the front portico, watching.

"Jessica," Lord Pembroke said in a distracted voice as he caught sight of Elizabeth. "In all the commotion, I quite forgot you would be arriving. You're welcome to stay, of course. But there's been an unfortunate incident. I'm not certain when I may be able to speak with you."

"What's happened?" Elizabeth asked.

Instead of answering, Pembroke placed a hand on her shoulder. Elizabeth was surprised to feel it trembling.

"Jessica," he said. "See that you don't mention today's, er, event to anyone at the newspaper— including that sister of yours. It is the subject of a police investigation, so any publicity at this time would be inappropriate." He spoke quietly, but his voice held a note of thinly disguised panic.

"Oh, you can count on me," Elizabeth assured him. "But I will stay, if you don't mind. Can you tell me what's—"

Before she finished speaking, Pembroke had turned away, satisfied, and was hurrying toward Constable Atherton, who was awaiting him near the ambulance with her arms folded impatiently in front of her.

Elizabeth approached the house and skirted the row of parked police cars. As she neared the clustered servants, she saw that most of them were weeping. "What in the world is going on?" she asked under her breath. "And is it related to the deaths of Joy and the others?"

She quickly decided on a course of action. After she learned what had just happened, she would slip inside the manor house and search for clues about the werewolf's identity and the Pembrokes' part in the murders.

Two servants passed close to where Elizabeth stood behind a hedge. ". . . found murdered this morning," she heard one of them say, before the couple moved out of earshot.

"Who was found murdered?" Elizabeth asked herself, out loud.

A moment later, she had her answer. Alistair, the tall, thin butler who had served tea on the morning of Joy's death, was led, sobbing, out of the house. Behind him, two paramedics carried a stretcher bearing what Elizabeth knew was a sheet-covered corpse. The constable lifted the sheet, and Elizabeth gasped.

On the stretcher lay the body of the Pembrokes' pretty, brown-haired cook, Maria Finch. Even from a distance, Elizabeth could see on her throat a bright red gash.

Chapter 7

Eliana took a dripping saucepan from David on Tuesday afternoon and began rubbing it with her dish towel.

"Working at the shelter's soup kitchen with you today has been just super, Lina," David said, plunging his hands back into the soapy water. "So many people are less fortunate than we are. Nothing can compare to the feeling of knowing you've helped people who are down on their luck."

Eliana grinned. As she had told Elizabeth the night before, David was different from any boy she had ever dated. She tried to imagine self-centered Harry Camden, the prime minister's nephew, rolling up his cuff-linked sleeves to scrub pots in a soup kitchen. The image wouldn't come.

"I feel the same way about working with the poor," Eliana said, taking a large skillet from him. "Someday, I'd like to do something for them that's bigger than this—something that would make a real difference in people's lives."

David nodded solemnly. "The need is there, certainly. I served lunch to a woman with a broken arm. And to a man with cataracts. And to a little boy who couldn't stop coughing. Do these people have any means of receiving free medical services?"

"Not in this neighborhood," Eliana said with a sigh. "The nearest clinic is more than a dozen blocks away. I remember an announcement, at the opening ceremonies for this shelter, that a clinic was being planned, as well. But the funding fell through."

"That's a shame!" David said. Eliana felt a warm rush of love at the sincerity in his voice. "You know, Lina, if I had a lot of money, I would use it to fund the facilities for proper medical treatment for these people. And then instead of studying literature, I would put myself through medical school, so I could administer the treatment myself."

Then he looked at her curiously. "But Lina," he said, confused, "did you just say you were at the opening ceremonies for this shelter? That was several years ago. I thought this was your first visit to London."

Eliana chastised herself for the slip. Her mother considered her too young to be the royal family's representative at such events as the ribbon-cutting ceremony at the city's new homeless shelter—though it was one of the few royal duties she would have relished. But in this case, she had accompanied her older sister, Gloria, who despised such events. Of course, she couldn't let David know she had been there.

"Oh, I wasn't actually there!" she said breezily, keeping her eyes on the soup tureen she was drying. "One of the managers here told me about the ceremony. I would have been back in Liverpool at the time of it, of course."

"Ahh, Liverpool," David said, looking almost satisfied with her explanation. "I used to help out occasionally at a shelter there. Perhaps you know of it—it's not far from the Lime Street station—"

"Oh, I'm certain that I don't know it," Eliana interrupted. "My mother is quite overprotective. She would never allow me to work in this sort of place at home. That's one of the reasons I left, really." *At least, I'm not lying to him about that much.*

David's handsome face took on a thoughtful expression. "It's unfortunate that your mother feels that way," he said. "Helping people who are in need is just about the most important thing in the world. That's why I'd like to use my skills someday to treat the illnesses of the poor and the homeless."

Eliana looked at him admiringly. "The other young people I know who aspire to medical school are planning to specialize in diseases of the rich. What an empty life that would be."

"Most people think I'm insane!" David replied bitterly. "They tell me how much more money I could make in a specialty like plastic surgery." He gazed deep into her eyes. "But not you, Lina. That's what I love about you. You're so down-to-earth."

Eliana's breath caught at the word *love*. David hadn't exactly said he loved her, but he had come close. Part of her longed to hear him use those words, and then to repeat them back to him. On the other hand, the very thought of it sent her into a panic. Was she leading David on? Did she have any right to become this close to a boy she knew would hate her when he learned the truth about her?

David began to place his hands on her shoulders as though he was about to kiss her on the lips. Then he remembered the soapy dishwater that dripped from his fingers, and stopped, laughing. He leaned over to kiss her lightly on the forehead, holding his wet hands away from her.

"We're almost finished here," he said. "What do you say we spend the rest of the day sight-seeing together? Have you been to the Portobello Road flea market? We ought to make use of the free afternoon. Two working-class blokes from Liverpool don't often get the chance to explore the big city."

Elizabeth stood in Robert's room at Pembroke Manor on Tuesday afternoon, feeling guilty about prowling around his bedroom. *Maybe I should have just stayed in London,* she thought.

Elizabeth sighed, impatient with her own indecision. She had been thinking in circles all day—ever since the phone call to Lord Pembroke that morning. His gratitude toward Jessica made her feel reluctant sympathy toward the father and son. Maybe she was totally off base, suspecting them of murder. But then she remembered the odd way Lord Pembroke had ended their telephone conversation.

"I want you to know that Robert loves you very

much," he had said. "*Please remember that—no matter what happens.*"

No matter what happens? "What does that mean?" she asked herself aloud, for the tenth time that day. "Does it mean that Lord Pembroke is protecting his son? Is young Robert Pembroke a serial murderer—and a werewolf?"

She felt a prickling along her spine and was grateful that Jessica was not planning to see Robert that day. *And after today, I might have enough evidence to keep her from seeing him ever again.*

The scene that had taken place in front of the mansion a half hour earlier played back in Elizabeth's mind. Most of all, she remembered the sight of Alistair's slender shoulders shaking with anguished sobs as Maria's body was brought out of the house. The recollection of the cook's body helped Elizabeth steel herself for prying into Robert's belongings. She had to know, beyond any doubt, if he had killed Maria and the other victims.

As Elizabeth prepared to search the room for clues, the question she had tried to banish from her mind suddenly shoved its way to the forefront. Was Maria dead because of Elizabeth's investigation? Had somebody discovered that the servants had spoken to her? Perhaps the werewolf had seen Maria at the end of the upstairs corridor, just after the murder. Or perhaps Robert—or whoever the murderer was—had been outside the kitchen door, listening to every word of Elizabeth's interrogation of the servants. Was it her fault that Maria was dead?

She shook her head. "I won't think about that

103

right now," she whispered. "The most important thing now is to prove who the murderer is. If it's Robert Pembroke, something in this room ought to tell me that."

She started poking around Robert's spacious bedroom, unsure of exactly what she was searching for. But when she opened the door to the enormous walk-in closet, Elizabeth gasped. She finally had her proof.

Hanging inside the closet door was a paisley-patterned silk bathrobe, in hunter green—with a small tear on one shoulder.

With trembling hands, Elizabeth removed the envelope from her backpack and pulled out the threads she had taken from the doorway at the murder scene. The bathrobe was a perfect match. Robert Pembroke had been in the room where Joy Singleton was murdered!

Elizabeth jumped at the sound of approaching footsteps. She shoved Robert's bathrobe into her backpack to study later, and ran out into the hallway, seconds before a white-haired chambermaid appeared.

"May I help you?" the maid asked in a distracted voice. Elizabeth saw tearstains on her face, and knew she was grieving for the murdered cook. "It's Miss Jessica Wakefield, isn't it?"

"That's right," Elizabeth said, trying to control her excited breathing. She smiled tentatively, showing the dimple in her left cheek. "I'm afraid I'm lost in this big house," she said solemnly. "Can you direct me to, uh, the library?"

The library was the first thing that popped into

Elizabeth's head, and she wanted to kick herself as soon as she said it. Nobody who knew Jessica would believe she was searching for a library.

Elizabeth let out a sigh of relief as the maid gave her directions. *Of course, nobody here knows Jessica well enough to be suspicious of a statement like that.*

When Elizabeth pushed open the double doors to the library, she gazed admiringly at the huge, well-stocked room. She closed the doors behind her carefully and began wandering around the ceiling-high shelves, reading the titles. As always, Elizabeth was fascinated by books.

Like every room at Pembroke Manor, the Pembroke library was richly decorated in a style Elizabeth thought of as very English. This room had a masculine look, with a big mahogany desk in one corner and accents of burgundy leather everywhere. Grouped on the desk and arranged on one wall was a collection of formal family portraits in gilt-edged wood frames.

She stood for a moment in front of the wall of portraits. The largest was a studio photograph of Robert, standing in the full riding attire that Jessica had described from her first meeting with him. He looked just as he always did to Elizabeth—handsome, smug, and self-important.

But the books were what held Elizabeth's attention. She pulled out a copy of *Wuthering Heights*—a first edition, she was sure—and lovingly fingered its well-dusted leather spine. Then she pushed it back onto the shelf, forcing herself to remember her mission. She began looking for clues.

When she saw Robert Louis Stevenson's *The Strange Case of Dr. Jekyll and Mr. Hyde,* Elizabeth forgot her resolve once more. She had started to read the book last week at HIS and hadn't had a chance to get back to it since. Well, Pembroke had told her to make herself at home. Perhaps he wouldn't mind if she borrowed it for the evening, to read in bed. She reached up and began to pull the book from the shelf.

Elizabeth heard a loud click. She whirled guiltily, and her eyes widened with astonishment. A leather-covered panel in the wall had sprung open. Pulling out the volume had triggered a secret door!

"Even the walls here aren't what they seem," she whispered breathlessly.

Then Elizabeth pushed open the secret door and walked slowly into the small, dark room.

Jessica sighed dramatically. "But what's wrong with my sentence?" she asked, jabbing at Tuesday's Bumpo story on her computer screen. "It says 'the man who was arrested stole a single shoe from each of seventeen women!' What right do you have to make me change it?"

"Don't be angry at me," Luke said. "You know Tony asked me to help you with your article, in Elizabeth's absence. Actually, I think you've done a fine job, except that you can't say the man stole the shoes, because you don't know that for sure."

"Yes, I do," Jessica said. "I heard him tell Sergeant Bumpo he likes clogs the best—with platform heels. Face it, the guy is loony tunes. Even

Sergeant Bumpo says he's definitely the thief."

"He probably is," Luke conceded. "Nonetheless, you can't say so in the newspaper before he's been convicted of the crime. Until then, you have to say he's *suspected* of stealing the shoes."

Jessica sighed again. Life wasn't fair. She should be out in the country, covering a story within dropping-in distance of Pembroke Manor. And Elizabeth should be sitting here, listening to Luke tell her what's wrong with her article.

Of course, she admitted to herself, if Elizabeth had written it, there probably wouldn't be anything wrong with it. Jessica knew that writing wasn't her greatest talent. Still, it was humiliating to be told she needed a tutor. Besides, she was still mad at Elizabeth for hating Robert, so by extension, she was mad at her sister's boyfriend, too.

Jessica's only consolation was the knowledge that Elizabeth would get stuck with the Bumpo stories tomorrow, while Jessica and Robert drove out to Stonehenge, alone, in his silver convertible. She'd like to see the look on Elizabeth's face tomorrow, when she realized Jessica wasn't going to accompany her to the newspaper. She hoped Bumpo would dig up something particularly trivial and ridiculous to be reported on in Wednesday's *Journal.*

"I trust Robert has been showing you some of the high points of our fair country," Luke said after Jessica had sent the computer file to be printed. Jessica was surprised by his amiable tone.

"Yes," she boasted. "As a matter of fact, we're driving into the countryside tomorrow, to visit

Stonehenge—just the two of us, alone in the country!"

"You seem to have become very close to Robert in a short time," Luke said.

Jessica smiled, thinking of Robert. "Yes, I have," she answered happily. "I haven't felt this way about anyone in a long time. Consider me officially in love!"

"And does Robert return your feelings?" Luke asked, looking at her intently.

Jessica nodded. "Of course he does." Then she wrinkled her forehead. "Elizabeth didn't ask you to give me a big-brotherly talk about why I shouldn't love Robert, did she?"

Luke laughed, but his eyes looked troubled. He absentmindedly pulled a silver key chain from his pocket and began drumming it on the desk. "No—though I have to admit that the Pembrokes are not my favorite family."

Jessica bristled.

"Don't be upset, Jessica. I promise not to get big brotherly."

Jessica stared at him for a moment, until she was satisfied that he was telling the truth. Then she noticed his key chain and pointed to it. "Hey, that looks just like that weird necklace you gave Elizabeth. Do you really believe that werewolf stuff, or are you just putting my sister on?"

Luke laughed, then said, "I've been studying werewolves for a long time, Jessica. My mother was sort of an enthusiast; she got me interested when I was a small child. And after all these years of study, I've reached the conclusion that werewolves really do exist."

He gazed at her intently, and even Jessica had to admit that his startlingly blue eyes had a sexy, almost hypnotic quality. Then Luke recited in a solemn voice:

> "Through darkened wood he runs alone;
> White teeth gleam like sharpened bone.
> Wolfsbane bloom is softly kissed
> By moonlight drifting through the mist.
> By day he wishes no one ill;
> At night he hungers for the kill."

Jessica felt a shiver run down her spine, as if she ought to be looking over her shoulder. "Did you write that?"

Luke smiled, looking perfectly normal again. "Well, yes," he admitted. "But I'm still working on it, really. Do you like it?"

Jessica hesitated, uncertain. "It's kind of spooky."

"Good. It's supposed to be."

Suddenly, Jessica thought she knew what Luke was up to. She shook her finger at him. "I get it! You're trying to scare my sister so you can play the big, strong boyfriend. Well, you don't have to worry about me. I won't tell her your secret; I'm not even speaking to her."

"No, Jessica. It's not like that—"

"I don't know why Elizabeth is such a wimp all of a sudden," Jessica continued, "but I don't scare so easily. You poets are too weird. I'm just glad I'm dating a *normal* guy."

Chapter 8

Elizabeth groped for a light switch and stared around her. The secret room was a small, book-lined study.

Animal skins and heads adorned the walls, as in the dining room. But the dining-room animals were from African safaris. The animals in this room were wolves, leering down at her with their teeth bared.

"The wolves' den!" she whispered, spooked.

The room was stuffy, but Elizabeth shivered.

She caught sight of some of the titles of the leather-bound books, and her mouth dropped open. It seemed that every book in the room had something to do with werewolves. She suppressed a shudder. "Lord Pembroke must be some kind of werewolf fanatic," she whispered, more because of the eeriness of the room than out of a fear of being discovered. "How creepy!"

Then she remembered that Luke was also a serious student of werewolf lore. But, she told herself loyally, there was nothing creepy about Luke's fascination with the subject—not like Lord Pembroke's obsession. Collecting werewolf books and wolf heads and hiding them in a secret room was downright weird.

Still, Elizabeth had to admit that Luke would love this place. She couldn't wait to tell him about it.

For a moment, Elizabeth considered calling him. She eyed the telephone that sat on a small, cluttered desk in the center of the room. Then she shook her head. Her time for searching for clues was too limited to spend it talking on the phone; she would tell Luke later. But she did notice that the phone number was not the one she had used to call Pembroke that morning. The werewolf room was so secret it even had its own telephone number. She wondered if that was to keep people from picking up other extensions in the house and hearing Pembroke's private conversations.

Elizabeth turned to the crowded bookshelves and scanned the titles. Unlike the well-kept volumes in Lord Pembroke's main library, most of the books in the werewolf room were blanketed with a layer of dust. Obviously, not even the servants knew about this room.

Elizabeth selected a beautifully bound volume, a sixteenth-century French work called *Discours de la Lycanthropie*. "Discourses on Lycanthropy," she translated aloud. Before coming to England, she had never heard of lycanthropy. Now, she knew the term was used both for the study of werewolves and for the delusion that a person has turned into a wolf. The book fell open in Elizabeth's hands. She blew the fine powder from the title page and read an inscription written in graceful, elongated script: "To Robert. With all my love, Annabelle."

The inscription was dated twenty years earlier, so Elizabeth knew the words had been written to the elder Lord Pembroke, rather than his son. "But who is Annabelle?" she asked aloud. The inscription sounded as if it had been written by a lover—but certainly Lord and Lady Pembroke had been married at the time; Robert was twenty years old.

But Lady Pembroke's first name was not Annabelle.

Elizabeth's imagination began to race. Had Lord Pembroke and Annabelle had a tragic love affair, twenty years earlier? Was that the scandal Eliana had mentioned? And where was Annabelle now?

For a moment, Elizabeth felt a twinge of sympathy for Lord Pembroke, but she pushed it aside, chastising herself for being too sentimental. She was here to solve a mystery and capture a killer, not to moon over a twenty-year-old romance.

Elizabeth stared thoughtfully at the inscription. "Could Annabelle be the key to the mystery?" she asked herself aloud.

Elizabeth didn't know, but she was determined to find the answers.

"Earth to Lina and David!" Emily called, waving her hand between her two friends' faces, as a group of HIS residents sat on the front steps of the dormitory Tuesday evening. "Stop gazing longingly into each other's eyes for a moment, will you? We have serious business to discuss."

Eliana and David both blushed.

"You're both about as red as that double-decker bus that just passed by!" Gabriello Moretti said gleefully, pretending to play a cadence with a pair of imaginary drumsticks. "I suppose that means you had a pleasant afternoon." He winked at Rene.

Eliana blushed again. "So, Emily, what's this important business we have to discuss?"

"We must determine what we're going to do tonight, of course. I'm as bored as a kangaroo in a body cast. How about it, Jessica? You're always a good one for ideas."

Jessica shrugged her shoulders. "I don't know."

"Where's Elizabeth tonight?" David asked.

Ooops, Emily thought. *Bad subject.*

Jessica grimaced. "Miss Newspaper Reporter is out in the countryside for the evening, covering the story of the century: 'Farmer Raises Flamingos.'"

"Ostriches," Eliana corrected.

Jessica stared at her. "How did you know about that? Tony didn't approve the story until today."

Eliana shrugged innocently. "Elizabeth told me last night that she was going to ask Tony if she could write about them."

"Whatever," Jessica said airily. Then Jessica bit her lip sadly, and Emily realized that Jessica missed her twin sister, despite their argument.

"And I suppose Portia has a performance of *A Common Man* tonight," Rene said.

"That's right," Eliana said. "So what shall the rest

of us do with ourselves tonight? I don't think we want to sit here on the steps all evening, complaining about how bored we are."

Emily snapped her fingers. "I have an idea! I've heard about a posh comedy club in Soho. The admission's supposed to be a little pricey, but it'll be worth it. The place is called Comic-kazi."

"That won't work," Eliana said offhandedly. "Comic-kazi is closed on Tuesdays."

Emily stared at her, surprised that Lina would be so familiar with the fashionable London club. This wasn't the first time the working-class girl from Liverpool had revealed a surprising knowledge of London society. Emily noticed that David looked at Lina, too, his face full of anxiety.

"How did you know that, Lina?" Emily asked.

Eliana blushed again. "I suppose I must've read about it somewhere."

"Is anyone in the mood for a film?" Rene asked.

"I don't think so," Jessica said glumly.

"There aren't many good movies out that I haven't seen," Emily said.

"I've got it!" Gabriello said. "A friend of mine is in a band that's playing at the Pink Zebra tonight."

"The Pink Zebra?" David said. "Sounds trendy!"

Emily grinned. "It is! I've read about it in one of the tabloids—it's where the fashionable crowd goes when they feel a need for punking out!"

Even Jessica seemed to brighten.

But Eliana shifted uncomfortably on the concrete step. "I hope you have a wonderful time," she said, yawning. "But I think I'll bow out and get to bed early. I'm a bit tired all of a sudden."

Eliana jumped up from the step and disappeared into the dorm.

"What's with her?" Emily asked. "Just a few minutes ago, she was as eager to go out as any of us."

David sighed and shook his head. "I don't know," he said, almost in a whisper. "Sometimes I don't understand Lina at all."

Elizabeth leaned over Lord Pembroke's ornately carved mahogany desk early on Wednesday morning. Her search of the library and werewolf room had been interrupted the day before when a servant came to dust the library. Elizabeth had barely made it out of the hidden room in time.

She resolved to be more careful today. Elizabeth hadn't seen Lord Pembroke since her arrival the day before; she hoped he was still in bed that morning. Certainly, Maria's murder had made Pembroke forget all about the interview he was supposed to have with "Jessica" today. But that was fine with Elizabeth. She thought she had a better chance of finding something useful if she could manage some uninterrupted time for sleuthing around Pembroke Manor.

So far, Elizabeth's trip had been successful. The green robe was circumstantial evidence, but it did implicate Robert for Joy's murder. And the werewolf room was interesting, though Elizabeth wasn't sure how Lord Pembroke's obsession with werewolves tied in to the murders. What did it mean? Had Lord Pembroke known all along that his son was a werewolf? Was his study of lycanthropy an effort to understand more about Robert's condition? No, she decided. The date on Annabelle's gift book proved that Pembroke had been interested in werewolves at least since the time of Robert's birth. So what did it all mean?

Elizabeth sighed. Despite her discoveries, she still hadn't even found solid proof that the younger Robert Pembroke was a werewolf and a murderer. But time was running out; her train would leave for London in a few hours.

"Annabelle," she said aloud, thinking of the inscription on the werewolf book. "I don't know why, but I know she's important to all of this."

Elizabeth slowly opened the top drawer of Pembroke's desk and immediately saw what she was looking for—an address book.

"Annabelle," she said again, thumbing through the pages as quickly as she could. "Why couldn't Annabelle have signed her last name on her inscription, too?"

She laid the address book back in the drawer and sighed heavily. Of the entries that listed first names, not a single one mentioned an Annabelle. Then she turned and scrutinized the shelves until she saw what looked like a college yearbook. From the date on the spine, she guessed it was Pembroke's yearbook.

"Oxford," she said. "Naturally."

She flipped through the pages until she found his photograph.

"Lettered in crew and polo," she read. "Debating Society, Dramatics Society, Hunt Club."

Not much help there. Elizabeth leafed through the back section of the book, where several pages had

117

been left blank for signatures. She scanned the pages for the elegant, elongated handwriting she had memorized from the inscription in the werewolf book. There was no Annabelle.

"I guess I'll try the wolves' den one last time," she said under her breath, reaching for the copy of *Jekyll and Hyde* that she now knew would trigger the secret door.

As her fingers grazed the volume, Elizabeth froze. She could hear Lord Pembroke's voice, just outside the library doors.

Elizabeth dove under the mahogany desk as Pembroke strolled into the room, followed by Andrew Thatcher. Then she clapped her hand over her mouth in consternation—the secret door had clicked open and was standing slightly ajar. If Pembroke or Thatcher noticed it, they would surely discover her.

"Yesterday's murder was the last straw," Thatcher said after he had closed the double doors behind them. Elizabeth noticed that the police chief looked thinner and more haggard than just a couple days earlier; Joy's death was apparently taking its toll on him. "I know we agreed that the killer would be apprehended more quickly if we kept it out of the newspapers. And that due to your expertise you would, in a sense, carry on your own investigation." He ran his hand through his dark hair, making it stand on end. "But I can't risk any more lives, Robert. We have to bring this monster in. My detectives at Scotland Yard are breathing down my neck. They suspect that you know more than you're telling—and I think so, too."

Pembroke began pacing. Elizabeth held her breath as he approached the secret door; she let it out, relieved, as he passed by the door without stopping.

"Just a little more time, Andrew," Pembroke pleaded. "We've known each other since boyhood—trust me for a few more days. You know that we're onto something big here, but we can't afford to play our hand too early."

"We can't afford to wait!" Thatcher yelled. "Four people have died! How many more will it take? I know you have evidence of who it is—"

"But Andrew," Pembroke argued.

"Don't try to deny it," Thatcher said. "I've gone along with you until now, but no longer. I don't care how long we've been friends. Robert, I have to know what you know. Tell me who the evidence points to, and hand over any clues you have—regardless of who they implicate."

Pembroke shook his head nervously. "I don't think that's a good idea. The evidence I've found is misleading. It points to an innocent man!"

What evidence can he have? Elizabeth wondered, thinking of the large portrait of Robert on the wall. *Does Lord Pembroke suspect Robert, too?* Then she cringed as he passed near the partially open door to the werewolf room.

"That's what police investigations are for," Thatcher said. "You just hand over the evidence, and let us decide if it warrants an arrest. Don't worry. We'll have to be bloody sure of the evidence before we accuse a man of being a werewolf!"

Elizabeth's eyes widened. Pembroke and Thatcher

had known all along about the werewolf!

"But if I have all the evidence," Thatcher continued, "I can put out a warrant for the suspect's arrest. Then we can question him and arrive at the truth of the matter."

Pembroke sat down heavily in the desk chair, and Thatcher took over the pacing. Beneath the desk, Elizabeth scooted as far away from his knees as she could get, plastering her body against the opposite side. For a moment, Pembroke sat with his elbows on the mahogany surface, cradling his forehead in his hands.

"All right," he said reluctantly, his voice muffled. "I'll turn over the evidence. But not right now. Let me talk to him first." He hesitated. "Perhaps I can coax him to quietly turn himself in for questioning— although, as I told you, I'm certain he's innocent."

He pushed the chair out from the desk and turned to Thatcher. The police chief stopped pacing and stood with his arms folded—directly in front of the door to the werewolf room.

Elizabeth stiffened, willing the police chief not to turn around and see that the leather-covered panel was slightly open.

"I'll allow you until ten o'clock tonight to give me the evidence," Thatcher said. "But that's it! If you can convince your friend to turn himself in, then perhaps the law will go easier on him. But if you even think about changing your mind, Robert, remember that I can subpoena you to turn over any evidence you've found."

Pembroke nodded wordlessly.

"Our friendship is important to me, Robert," Thatcher said. "But you know I could lose my job if anyone finds out I've been allowing you to withhold evidence."

"I understand, Andrew. And I appreciate your co-operation. You're a good friend."

Thatcher strode across the room to the double doors of the library and then turned to face Pembroke again. "Do me a favor, Robert," he said. "Tell Reeves to ease up on the princess hype. It's making us look like we're not doing our job!"

After the police chief had left, Lord Pembroke stood in front of Robert's portrait. "The evidence must be wrong," he said in a determined voice. "My son is not a killer—or a werewolf! I refuse to believe it. I'll clear your name, Robert," he vowed, eyes fierce with determination. "I promise I will."

Lord Pembroke stared up at his son's portrait, slowly shaking his head. Robert was innocent. Of that, he had no doubt.

Perhaps he was misinterpreting the evidence he'd found—the cigarette case from the Essex Street murder site and the green threads from Robert's silk bathrobe. Or perhaps someone else had planted the evidence, in order to frame his son. But who would do such a thing? And why?

The only thing he knew for sure was that he couldn't let the police arrest his son. Robert was no murderer. And Pembroke had promised himself years earlier that he would never let another scandal rock the Pembroke family name.

"I must warn Robert before I talk to Thatcher,"

he decided aloud. "He must disappear for a bit—allow me time to find the real werewolf."

He reached across the desk for the telephone, but then changed his mind. For this call, he needed the complete privacy of his hidden room, with its separate phone line. It would never do for a bumbling servant to happen upon him at an inopportune point in the conversation. *Too many people are investigating this case already,* he told himself, thinking about Jessica Wakefield's nosy sister scribbling in that notebook of hers. He would make the call from his secret study.

Pembroke reached for *The Strange Case of Dr. Jekyll and Mr. Hyde* to trigger the hidden door. Then he froze. The leather-covered panel was already open.

"That's odd," he said aloud, fighting down a feeling of panic. "I'm certain I didn't leave that door ajar." But nobody else even knew of the existence of the wolf den—not even his wife. "Annabelle is the only other soul who ever knew about this room, and that was years ago."

He stood in the doorway and gazed around his private study. Nothing seemed to have been disturbed. In fact, he felt the same rush of emotion that always engulfed him upon entering the secret room—an odd mixture of security, mystery, and passion. He and Annabelle had spent so many happy hours there, examining old documents and discovering new theories.

But the concerns of the present were too disturbing to allow more than a moment of nostalgia.

Somebody else had discovered his room. Perhaps one of the servants had pulled out *Jekyll and Hyde* while dusting, he told himself. He would have to investigate—after he called Robert.

He closed the hidden door carefully behind him as he walked into the little room.

Lord Pembroke had another mystery on his hands.

As soon as Lord Pembroke disappeared into the secret study, Elizabeth jumped out from under the mahogany desk and raced from the library. She leaped up the stairs, two at a time, to reach the telephone in the hallway outside her room. The information she had just overheard couldn't wait; she had to call Luke right away and fill him in on everything she had learned. It was lucky that the telephone Lord Pembroke was using in the werewolf den was on a separate line.

Elizabeth tapped her foot impatiently as the phone rang repeatedly on Luke's desk at the *Journal*.

"Rats!" she said aloud. "Where could he be?"

She dialed Tony's number instead.

"I'm not completely certain where Luke is this morning, Liz," Tony replied to her urgent question. "Out and about on an arts and entertainment scoop, no doubt. I've actually been able to get a lot of work done, with you and Luke out on your various stories, and Jessica spending the day with that young nobleman of hers—"

Elizabeth broke out in a cold sweat. *"Jessica is where?"*

123

"I assumed you knew," Tony said. "She took a holiday today to spend some time with the young Lord Pembroke. She didn't mention where they would be going."

Elizabeth's hands were trembling as she replaced the telephone receiver. Jessica was alone all day with a killer—and probably a werewolf!

Elizabeth knew she had to return to London immediately. She had to find Jessica—before it was too late.

Chapter 9

"They think you're the werewolf," Lord Pembroke told his son over the phone Wednesday morning. "I know you're not, of course, but soon the situation will be out of my control."

Robert's voice over the phone sounded impatient and a bit smug. "I didn't think anything was out of the control of the Pembroke family. Besides, the police have no proof against me."

"They will, soon," Pembroke replied ominously. "Thatcher has threatened to subpoena me if I don't tell him everything I know by ten o'clock tonight."

"I believe you're overreacting, Father."

"Overreacting? You don't seem to understand, Robert. The police will believe you are a serial killer and a werewolf. They'll put out a warrant for your arrest. And the newspapers will have a field day. There will be a horrible scandal, even if they determine there isn't enough evidence to bring you to trial."

"And what would you have me do, Father?"

"We can't let Thatcher's people bring you in for questioning. I must clear your name."

"How do you propose to do that?"

"I probably know more about werewolves than any living person in England. If anyone can track down the real werewolf, I can. Until then, I want you to disappear for a few days. Get out of town this morning—now!"

"I'm afraid that's not possible. I have plans for this morning. I'm—"

"Change your plans," Pembroke interrupted. "I'll get word to you when it's safe to return."

"All right, Father, if you insist. But I can't depart immediately, Father. I'd planned to meet somebody shortly—and our appointment is even more crucial, now that I know the police will be after me soon. I'll leave town as soon as I've finished."

Jessica jumped into the passenger seat of Robert's silver Jaguar.

"Why's the top up?" she asked, after kissing him good morning. "The London weather is actually cooperating, for a change. What's the use of having a convertible if you can't take advantage of a little good weather?"

"How are you this morning, Jessica?" Robert asked formally.

Jessica looked at Robert curiously. He seemed awfully distracted. His eyes hadn't even lingered on the outfit she'd chosen especially for the occasion—a short, breezy dress that showed off her shoulders and exactly matched the turquoise color of her eyes.

Well, Jessica knew the cure for a distracted boyfriend. A little bit of bright chatter would cheer him up right away—especially when combined with the prospect of spending the day together out in the country, just the two of them. She was confident that he would notice her outfit in no time.

"I'm so relieved to have the day off from that boring newspaper!" Jessica exclaimed. "Yesterday's story, the Case of the Clog Robber, just about did me in. You don't know how much I've been looking forward to our trip to Stonehenge today!"

Robert sighed, keeping his eyes focused on the road ahead of him. "I'm afraid there's been a change of plans," he said. "Let's go to the Connaught, shall we? I'll fill you in over breakfast."

Jessica felt her heart sinking. She rode the rest of the way in silence.

Jessica poked her fork at the uneaten eggs Benedict on her plate. She couldn't believe that Robert was canceling their date—and that he was leaving town.

"But where are you going?" she asked. "How long will you be gone?"

"I don't know," Robert said, reaching across the table to take her hand. "But you'll have to look out for yourself until I return. Unfortunately, I may not be able to contact you."

"Why not?"

Robert ignored her question. "Don't worry. As soon as I get back, I'll find you."

"Get back from where?"

"I can't tell you that. Just promise me you'll be careful while I'm away."

Jessica looked into his eyes and saw an intensity there that frightened her. "Robert, none of this makes any sense! It's bad enough that my sister's turned into a basket case. Now you're getting all paranoid on me, too!"

Robert shook his head. "It's not like that, Jessica. But I can't go into the particulars."

"Are you in some kind of trouble? Let me help you!"

"There's nothing you can do," he told her. "Just promise me you'll be careful!"

Jessica shrugged, unable to resist his intense gaze. "All right, Robert. I'll be careful." *Is everyone in England crazy?* she wondered, remembering a snatch of an old song about mad dogs and Englishmen.

Robert glanced at his expensive watch. "I'm in a terrible hurry, Jessica. Here's enough money to pay the breakfast bill and to take a cab anywhere in the city that you want to go. If anyone asks, tell them you didn't see me this morning."

He tossed a few notes on the table in front of her, and kissed her with an urgency that was disturbing—almost frightening.

Then Jessica watched sadly as Robert—the only guy she'd loved since Sam's untimely death—hurried away from her.

128

❖   ❖   ❖

Elizabeth practically leapt off the train as soon as it pulled into Victoria Station.

"The customary procedure, miss," said an amused porter, "is to wait until the train has stopped before disembarking."

Elizabeth barely heard him as she ran toward a bank of telephones, all of which were in use. She shifted anxiously from one foot to the other as she waited for one of the callers to finish up.

My sister is in terrible danger! she wanted to scream. *Please let me use the phone.*

Elizabeth blamed herself. It was true that she had tried to warn her sister about the Pembrokes; Jessica wouldn't pay attention. But she should have tried harder.

She wished she had been able to get hold of Luke at the *Journal* that morning. Maybe he was back from his assignment by now. *Maybe he's seen Jessica—or knows where Robert was taking her!*

"Thank goodness for Luke," Elizabeth said under her breath. "I could never handle this alone."

A minute later, she was on the phone with Tony at the newspaper.

"Sorry, Liz. Luke isn't back yet. How are your ostrich friends?"

"Huh?"

"You know, the ostriches. The story you traveled all that distance for."

"Oh, fine, Tony. What about Jessica? Have you heard anything from her?"

"Well, no, Liz. But she's on a date with her beau. I

129

hardly would expect her to check in with me. Is something wrong? You sound rather distraught."

After she hung up the phone, Elizabeth stood for a moment with her hand on the receiver, contemplating her next move.

"The police!" she said aloud. Her sister was with a murderer. Obviously, she should call the police. She lifted the receiver, but quickly dropped it. Andrew Thatcher was the only person on the police force who would believe her story, and he hadn't returned to London yet.

She could just imagine herself saying to anyone else on the police force: "Excuse me, Officer, but I need your help. My sister's in terrible danger. You see, she has this date with a werewolf."

No, the police weren't an option. With Luke unreachable, she would have to rescue Jessica all by herself. But first, she had to find her.

"When the going gets tough, the tough go shopping," Jessica said aloud, standing in front of Harrods as her taxicab pulled away from the curb.

She still couldn't believe Robert had canceled their excursion to Stonehenge; she had been eager to spend some time alone with him, far away from the distractions of the city and the prying eyes of her nosy sister.

Even more disturbing was Robert's evasiveness. Why was he leaving town so suddenly? Where was he going? And why couldn't he answer any of her questions?

For a moment, she wondered if Robert could be some sort of secret agent, on a dangerous mission. "Nah," she decided, dismissing the notion almost as soon as it occurred to her. The idea appealed to her sense of adventure, but it was almost as farfetched as Elizabeth's fears about werewolves. At least one Wakefield had to hang on to her senses.

To make matters worse, the clear sky of early morning was now shrouded in gray storm clouds. It looked as if it would rain again, after all.

Well, Jessica had always prided herself on her resourcefulness. She hadn't had a minute to hit Harrods since she'd arrived in London—thanks to her stupid internship at the *Journal*. Now was her chance. And Robert had made the opportunity even more tempting, by leaving her with a little money to spare after she had covered the restaurant bill and cab fare.

Jessica pushed open the door of Harrods solemnly, as if she were entering a temple. She sighed, feeling lonely for the first time since she'd arrived in England. *Lila Fowler, where are you when I need you?*

Immediately, Jessica was drawn, as if by a magnet, to a department full of high-class European fashions. A black-and-white culotte set beckoned from the rack.

If shopping wouldn't cheer her up, nothing would.

"I'm looking for a sixteen-year-old blond girl—" Elizabeth began frantically, speaking with a street vendor that afternoon, just outside of Kensington Gardens.

"Aren't we all?" the college-age boy replied with a sardonic grin.

"She looks just like me."

The vendor took in her size-six figure and long golden hair. "This is sounding better and better," he said with a wink.

Elizabeth stifled the urge to slap him. Instead, she turned and ran into the gardens.

Ever since Elizabeth had gotten off the train at Victoria Station, she had been racking her brain to think of places Jessica wanted to see in London but hadn't been to yet. Where in London would Robert and Jessica go on their date?

Elizabeth's first stop had been Bond Street, to see if her sister was window-shopping at any of the high-class stores. Jessica and Robert could even be doing some real shopping, Elizabeth realized, remembering the size of Robert's family fortune. Jessica would be thrilled to bring back a souvenir worthy of anything Lila Fowler owned. But the store clerks Elizabeth spoke to hadn't seen Jessica and Robert. If Jessica had succumbed to her addiction for buying clothes she couldn't afford, she hadn't done it on Bond Street.

Now Elizabeth was in the biggest park in the city—and a park with a palace in it, to boot. And, Elizabeth realized, it was a perfect place for a romantic stroll. She hurried along the garden path, peering down the long rows of sculpted shrubberies that branched off to both sides. It was a weekday, so the gardens weren't crowded. She could just imagine Jessica and Robert walking hand in hand between the manicured hedges, in a secluded part of the park— *when suddenly Robert turned to Jessica, and blood dripped from his fangs. . . .*

"Stop it!" Elizabeth said to herself, aloud. A woman pushing a baby stroller looked at her curiously and steered a wide path around her.

Elizabeth took a deep breath and wrenched her mind away from dramatic images of Jessica in danger. "I have to be calm and objective," she told herself under her breath.

She wished Luke were there, but she had called the newspaper again, from Bond Street, and he still hadn't returned from his assignment. She would try again soon, but for now she was still on her own for finding Jessica—if it wasn't already too late.

She noticed Kensington Palace up ahead and remembered how eager Jessica had been to visit it. Several members of the royal family were living in Kensington Palace, but parts of it were open for tours. Elizabeth was sure the royals wouldn't hang out with the tourists, but it would be just like Jessica to expect to see a princess or two—or better yet, a prince.

Elizabeth allowed herself a moment of irony: *Won't Jessica be surprised to learn she's been sharing a room with a real, live princess all this time?*

She prayed that her sister would live long enough to hear all about it.

"You look as if you're attempting to buy out the

whole store!" a young salesclerk exclaimed as Jessica lugged her shopping bags to a checkout counter in Harrods, clutching a lovely silk scarf that would go perfectly with the chic purple minidress she'd bought a few minutes earlier.

"I guess I am on a serious power-shopping binge," Jessica replied. "I'm trying to drown my troubles in store receipts."

Once again, she handed the clerk the credit card the twins' parents had given them for this trip—in case of emergency. If this wasn't an emergency, Jessica didn't know what was. Within the first half hour, she'd spent the rest of the money Robert had left. Since then, she'd been working on the credit card and hoping she hadn't reached its limit.

Besides buying overpriced European clothes, Jessica reflected while the clerk rang up the scarf, her only consolation was that Elizabeth must be back in town by now. *Maybe she's getting stuck with the latest Bumpo scoop, while I have the day off!*

Jessica's attention was caught by a display of Italian shoes. She sighed, knowing she was probably about to pay twice as much money as she would ever consider spending on a pair of shoes back home. But the medium-height heels with the violet panels of lizard-look leather would be perfect with her new minidress.

Suddenly, Jessica felt a prickling at the back of her neck. She had the distinct feeling that someone was watching her. For an instant, she plainly heard Robert's voice: *"Promise me you'll be careful."*

Jessica turned slowly, pretending to be engrossed in the shoe display, while she peered out of the corner of her eye. Nobody was there.

"It was just some nosy salesperson, spying on me," she speculated under her breath. "It's because I'm an American teenager trying on everything in the store."

Suddenly, Jessica was swept by a wave of depression. Even the shopping binge—usually one of her favorite activities—was leaving her feeling strangely empty.

She reviewed her mental list of whom she was mad at. She was ticked off at Elizabeth for interfering with her relationship with Robert. She was ticked off at Tony Frank for not letting her work on exciting, glamorous stories at the *Journal*. She was ticked off at the nasty English weather that stayed gray and rainy practically all the time. And she was ticked off at her parents for not being rich enough so that she could actually afford all this stuff she was buying.

Most of all, Jessica was ticked off at Robert for standing her up that morning and not explaining why. Nobody did that to Jessica Wakefield and got away with it. But Robert was getting away with it—and that made her ticked off with herself, for loving him so much that she would let him do this to her.

"He's hiding something from me," Jessica whispered. "And I don't like it one bit."

"What do you do when someone you care about is hiding something from you?" David asked Portia as the two walked toward HIS Wednesday afternoon. He was obviously trying to keep his voice sounding

135

casual, but Portia could tell he was quite upset.

The two teenagers had run into each other on their way home. David was finished with classes for the day. Portia had come from a matinee performance of *A Common Man* and had several hours to rest before the evening show.

"When you love somebody, you're supposed to be honest with them," David continued. "But Lina is hiding something from me, and I don't know what it is. She claims to be from Liverpool, but she changes the subject every time I bring it up, as if she's ashamed of it. And sometimes she says the oddest things—as if she's lived a very different life from the one I would imagine. There's something strange in her past, Portia, but she won't confide in me at all. Maybe she doesn't really care about me, after all."

"Sometimes people keep secrets from one another because they do care," Portia said slowly. She was talking about Lina, but it was her father's image that popped into her mind. "If Lina is hiding something, maybe it's because she's afraid you wouldn't approve if you knew the truth." *Just like my father wouldn't approve if he knew I was appearing in a play.*

"But it would be better to know the truth!" David argued. "If you really love someone, then finding out their secrets wouldn't change that."

"Wouldn't that depend on the secret?" Portia asked.

David walked silently for a few yards. "I suppose so," he said. "But I think I deserve to know what Lina is hiding from me—no matter what it does to

136

our relationship. She can't go on being dishonest with me, or the relationship doesn't stand a chance, anyhow!"

"If Lina is hiding something important, then I suspect she can't go on that way much longer," Portia said, realizing she was speaking about herself, as well. "A person can't hide behind a lie forever. The truth has a way of coming out eventually."

"So why doesn't she just tell me herself?"

"Perhaps she wants to tell you, but doesn't know how to broach the subject."

"Well, she'd better find a way," David said, pausing as they reached the front steps of the dormitory. "I love Lina, but I don't know how much longer I can continue in a relationship that's based on dishonesty."

"If you really love her, you should try to be patient with her," Portia urged. "But I suppose you're right. She can't hide from you forever—just as I can't hide from my father forever. I don't know if I've been of any help with your problem, David, but you've certainly helped me with mine. I've decided to find a way to tell Sir Montford Albert who Penelope Abbott really is. And I'm going to do it soon—while my father is in town this week. But I haven't the foggiest idea how."

The Knightsbridge tube station seemed strangely quiet as Jessica descended deeper and deeper underground. Of course, it wasn't yet rush hour, but Jessica was still surprised at the lack of activity on a Wednesday afternoon.

She maneuvered her bulky Harrods packages through the turnstiles. As she glanced down at the well-stuffed shopping bags, she felt a twinge of guilt about her high-priced shopping overdose.

"No way," she said under her breath. "I refuse to feel guilty about shopping. Robert abandoned me this morning. I deserved to have a fun day."

Then she sighed miserably, realizing that her day of shopping hadn't been the least bit fun.

Jessica walked along the yellow-tiled corridors to the train platform, listening to the echo of her footsteps through the dim, empty station. The platform was deserted. Jessica suppressed a shudder; the shadowy stillness made it easy to imagine that she was buried alive.

The silence seemed to wait, holding its breath. Jessica held her breath, too.

If I were skittish, she thought, *I'd call this eerie.* Elizabeth would probably call it eerie. But Elizabeth had turned into a paranoid chicken, after hearing a few of Luke's werewolf stories. Jessica was not paranoid. She forced herself to breathe normally, refusing to be scared by the fact that it was utterly silent in the cold, damp underground. Dead silent.

Suddenly, Jessica froze. A strange noise was coming out of the dark tunnel. It was a heavy, panting sound—definitely not the subway train.

And it was coming faster.

Jessica's eyes widened. She certainly wasn't going to wait around on the deserted platform to see if it was coming for her. She took off, running full speed down the platform, with her shopping bags bumping uncomfortably around her legs. She had to get away from the panting—away from something that was coming, faster and faster, out of the shadows. In a panic, she realized that the creature was rapidly catching up with her. She couldn't outrun it.

The panting was directly behind her. Jessica felt the creature's hot breath on the back of her neck.

Then she tripped and fell to the cold, tile floor.

Chapter 10

As Elizabeth raced through the door of the newspaper office on Wednesday afternoon, she plowed straight into Tony Frank, on his way out of the building in a rush.

"Sorry, Tony," she said breathlessly, as she helped him retrieve the notebook and tape recorder he'd dropped when she ran into him. "But I'm glad I caught you. I have to talk to you! It's urgent!"

"Not now, Elizabeth," he said brusquely. "Henry Reeves just informed me that a body was found at Pembroke Manor yesterday morning—there's no telling why the police didn't release the information yesterday. Not to mention Lord Pembroke himself. But I must head out there now to investigate."

Elizabeth opened her mouth to tell him Jessica's life was in danger, but Tony kept talking, in a frantic tumble of words.

"It's a nasty business, all right," he said. "Henry

heard a rumor that the dead woman might be Princess Eliana. So, as you can imagine, I've no time for a chat. Henry insisted that I write up a story, based on that rumor, so I have. But it would never do to run it in tonight's edition until it's substantiated. And nobody is willing to tell me anything over the phone."

He pushed past her and was about to rush out of the building, but Elizabeth's next words brought him to a halt.

"It's not the princess!"

Elizabeth's voice held such certainty that Tony turned to stare at her.

"It's not the princess," Elizabeth said again, feeling tears of frustration in her eyes. She was frantic about Jessica, and Tony was the only person she could turn to.

"I don't understand," he said. "How do you know it's not the princess?"

Elizabeth almost blurted out the whole story: *Because the princess is living in my dorm room and working in a soup kitchen.* But she stopped herself in time to keep Eliana's secret safe.

Elizabeth took a deep breath. "I was at Pembroke Manor yesterday morning when the body was carried out of the house. The dead woman is definitely not Princess Eliana. It's Maria Finch, the Pembrokes' cook. Please don't go, Tony. I've got to talk to you right now. It's about that murder, and another murder that could take place today if we don't stop it!"

Tony stared at Elizabeth for a moment, taking in her wide eyes and tense posture.

"All right," he said quietly, leading her back into

his office. "Let's hear what you have to say."

Jessica sprawled, facedown, on the cold floor of the subway platform, her fingers clenched around the handles of her forgotten shopping bags. Directly above her, something snarled; to Jessica, the noise seemed to echo off the vaulted ceilings, filling the deserted tunnels with terror and loathing.

Jessica tried to move, but her limbs wouldn't obey—as if she were paralyzed by fear in a nightmare that was terrifyingly real. The floor felt as cold as a tomb.

Something hairy brushed against the back of Jessica's arm. She stifled a scream. It was Elizabeth's werewolf. It had to be.

Jessica began to tremble. Hot breath seemed to singe the hairs on the back of her neck as the creature leaned over her. The panting filled her ears, like a sky full of thunder.

Then Jessica heard something else. Loud voices bounced off the walls of the corridors, coming closer. The heavy panting quieted to a low rumble, as if her attacker had stopped to listen.

"It's as if the firm were giving executives free lobotomies as a fringe benefit!" a man's voice boomed from a nearby corridor. A woman's voice responded: "Before they made her a vice president, Wanda was as reasonable as any of us—"

Then the hairy creature was gone. Through the pounding of her own pulse, Jessica vaguely heard it running away, down the empty platform.

For a moment, Jessica was too scared to move.

Then she picked herself and her shopping bags off the floor and dusted off her clothes. She was still alive. It hadn't gotten her.

Jessica stared around her wildly as she fought to catch her breath. Nobody, and no thing, was in sight. The hairy creature must have been swallowed up by the murkiness of the train tunnel.

She jumped at a harsh burst of laughter coming from behind her. But it was only a group of business-people in long raincoats, emerging onto the other end of the platform from the yellow-tiled corridor. The booming voice came from a tall man in a black bowler hat, who was loudly regaling the others with another anecdote about the new executive, Wanda.

Jessica wanted to ask the group for help, but she knew that her story would sound preposterous: *"A big hairy thing attacked me on the tube platform. It must be the werewolf my sister's been looking for."*

Instead, she shook her head and sighed loudly. Under her breath, she thanked the man with the bowler hat and the booming voice, for showing up when he did. He would never know it, but he had just saved her life.

Jessica's feud with her sister suddenly seemed unimportant. "I'll go to the newspaper office," she decided in a whisper, praying that Elizabeth and Luke would be there. "They're the werewolf hunters. They'll know what to do."

But the tube station was giving Jessica the creeps, after her encounter with her hairy assailant. She didn't think she could bear to wait there on the plat-form for the train; she would take a taxi instead.

Besides, it would be faster. She clumsily shifted a shopping bag from one hand to the other, to check her purse for the cab fare.

"Darn!" she said aloud, causing the man in the bowler hat to turn for a moment to look at her. Not only had her shopping spree topped the credit limit on her card, but it had also taken every last pence in her wallet.

Jessica had no choice now; she would have to wait for the subway. She edged closer to the cluster of people in raincoats, not daring to peer again into the depths of the murky train tunnel where she knew the hairy creature had disappeared.

But when she turned away from the tunnel, Jessica was gripped by terror. She imagined she still heard the panting behind her, and felt a pair of savage eyes boring hungrily into her back.

"You know, David really cares about you," Portia said to Eliana as the two girls sat down to tea in the dining room of HIS on Wednesday. "But he's upset. He thinks you don't trust him."

"I do trust David," Eliana said. "At least, I think I do."

"It's none of my business, Lina, but I hate to see a nice fellow like David get hurt. Besides, I think you love him, too. When you feel that way about someone, you should be honest with him."

Eliana's eyes glistened with sudden tears. "But what if David stops loving me when he knows what I really am?"

Portia was mystified. *What terrible secret can*

145

sweet, simple Lina be hiding? "David's not like that, Lina," she said gently. "You have to trust in his love for you, and let him know the truth—whatever it is."

"I could say the same thing about you and your father," Eliana reminded her.

Portia sighed. "My father doesn't care about the real me. He's made up his mind that I shouldn't be an actress, and that's that. He's so overprotective. I wish he would let me try myself, so I can succeed or fail on my own merits."

Eliana nodded her head. "I know what that's like. My mother is the *queen* of overprotection." She smiled enigmatically. "She barely lets me out of the pa—*house!*"

"That seems a bit extreme," Portia agreed.

"I guess it started when I was a baby," Eliana explained. "I was sick a lot, and I almost died once. So Mum's always been rather protective of me. To make matters worse, Glor—my older sister was kind of a swinger at my age. I suppose Mum's afraid I would be the same way if given the chance, even though my sister and I are nothing alike. I just wish she would trust me to make my own decisions."

Mrs. Bates bustled into the room. "Can I freshen your tea, Portia dear?" she asked, hovering over her.

"No, thank you, Mrs. Bates," Portia told her politely, annoyed at the interruption.

"I'll have some—" Eliana began, but the dorm mother didn't seem to hear her.

"Tell me, Portia, have you heard from your father lately? Did I tell you I saw him last year in *King Lear?*"

"Yes, you did, as a matter of fact—" Portia began, but the dorm mother kept talking.

"Sir Montford Albert! Now there's a fine figure of a man! Portia, dear, can I get you anything else to eat? I've got some lovely crumpets in the kitchen."

"No, thank you," Portia said, rolling her eyes at Eliana.

As soon as the door closed behind Mrs. Bates, Portia exploded. "I hate that!" she exclaimed. "Why do people treat you differently when they know you're 'upper class,' whatever that means? You know, that's one of the things I like about being Penelope Abbott. I want people to judge me by my actions, not my lineage." She sighed. "You don't know how lucky you are to be a normal person. But I guess that's hard for you to understand."

Eliana was staring at her intensely. "No, it's not," she said fervently. "I know exactly what you're talking about!" Then she softened her tone. "I mean, I notice the way Mrs. Bates and people like her act around you."

"I wish I didn't come from a famous family."

"But Portia," Eliana began slowly, as if she was just coming to a new realization. "Your lineage is part of you, too. More and more, I see that you can't hide who you really are. A person who really cares should accept you for the real you—all of you."

"So, are you going to trust David with the real you?"

"Yes," Eliana decided. Then she smiled, a little wistfully. "As soon as I can get up the nerve. Are you going to trust your father with the real Penelope Abbott?"

"Yes," Portia said, suddenly knowing exactly how to tell her father the truth about her. "And I'm going to do it today. I'm sending him tickets to tonight's performance of *A Common Man*. He's already judged me as his daughter. Now I want him to judge me as an actress."

Tony ushered Elizabeth into his office that afternoon and closed the door.

Elizabeth whirled to face him. "Has Jessica called in since the last time I talked to you?"

Tony shook his head impatiently. "You said you had urgent information about the murder, Liz! Do we have to waste time discussing your sister's social calendar?"

Elizabeth began pacing across the small office, terrified that Tony wouldn't believe her story. "This is about the murder," she said, her voice rising. "I think Jessica might be the next victim. We have to find her!"

"Whoa! Let's start at the beginning, shall we? Tell me what you know about the murder, and why you think Jessica is in danger. But first, stop that infernal pacing! You're making me dizzy."

Elizabeth perched nervously on the edge of his desk and told him about her investigation, beginning with eavesdropping outside the window of Cameron Neville's house more than a week earlier, and ending with Lord Pembroke's conversation in the library that morning.

A few minutes after she started, Luke walked into the office, looking for her. Elizabeth pecked him on

the cheek gratefully, feeling her confidence returning. She filled him in on everything she had seen and
heard since their last conversation—with the excep-
tion of the mysterious Annabelle, who had signed
Lord Pembroke's book, "With all my love." Elizabeth
still had no evidence that Annabelle was connected to
the murders, except her own gut feeling. She decided
she would tell Luke about the inscription later, when
Tony wasn't around.

"Well, I can't say that I believe the murderer is an
actual werewolf," Tony said at last. "Though I know
that the elder Lord Pembroke has been a bit of a
werewolf hobbyist for years. But it does sound as if
you could make a murder case against young Robert
Pembroke—if he's still in town. But, Liz, I still don't
understand about the cook's murder yesterday. You
say Pembroke was there. Why didn't he inform the
newspaper? Did he actually believe we wouldn't find
out?"

"I don't know what he believed. But he seemed
panicky when they carried the body out yesterday—
as if he wasn't thinking straight. And he specifically
warned me not to tell anyone at the *Journal* about
the murder."

Tony stared at her curiously. "So why are you
telling me now? How do you know I'm not in league
with Pembroke to cover up the murder stories?" He
looked down at his shoes. "Lucy Friday seems to believe I am."

Elizabeth shrugged. "I know we can trust you,"
she said. "Besides, I'm afraid for Jessica. I never
would have stayed at Pembroke Manor if I'd known

she was spending the day alone with Robert. He's a werewolf and a serial murderer! If anything happens to Jessica, it will be all my fault!"

Luke put a hand on her shoulder. "Nonsense, Liz. Until you overheard Pembroke and Thatcher this morning, you had no solid evidence that Robert could be dangerous. You can't blame yourself."

"Actually," Tony said, "I'd like to bring this to Lucy. She's angry at me, of course, but I'm sure we can put our squabbles aside for something this important. She was certain that the newspaper was intentionally covering up the earlier murders. And she's a more experienced investigator than any of us. I'd like to hear her take on what you've just told me."

"More talking?" Elizabeth asked, jumping from her seat. "Why are we wasting time talking? We've got to find Jessica!"

As she spoke, the door behind her opened.

"You've found her," Jessica announced from the doorway.

Elizabeth whirled in time to see an unwieldy load of shopping bags thud to the floor around her sister.

"Thank goodness you're all right, Jessica!" she exclaimed. "I thought you were in danger. I—"

Suddenly, she noticed her sister's sweat-streaked face and disheveled hair. Jessica's bare-shouldered turquoise dress was smudged with dirt. But the most disturbing thing of all was the terrified look in Jessica's blue-green eyes.

"You were right, Liz," Jessica began breathlessly. "It's after me! It attacked me in the Knightsbridge tube station. It chased me from behind. It was getting closer. Then I fell flat on my face, and I could feel it leaning over me."

"*What* attacked you?" Tony asked, disturbed.

Jessica shook her head. "I'm not sure. It was big— at least, it was bigger than me. And it made an awful kind of panting, growling, snarly noise."

She shuddered visibly. "I was wrong, Liz," she said. "I never dreamed I'd be saying this, but I am starting to believe in werewolves. Whatever attacked me was pretty hairy."

Chapter 11

Jessica settled gratefully into the overstuffed couch in Lucy's flat. It was only midafternoon Wednesday, but it had been a long, terrible day, and Jessica was exhausted.

Lucy rolled the green silk threads between her fingers. "So you found these in the door frame of the room where Joy Singleton was killed?"

Elizabeth nodded. "With the piece of fur."

"Do you know where the threads come from?"

Elizabeth nodded again, more nervously this time. She glanced over at Jessica, bit her lip, and unfolded a large piece of fabric from her backpack—the green paisley silk bathrobe.

Jessica gasped. "That belongs to Robert! What are you doing with it?"

"It looks like an exact match for the pieces of fiber I found in the door frame," Elizabeth explained, handing the robe to Lucy.

"Where did you get Robert's robe?" Jessica asked suspiciously.

"I took it from his closet at Pembroke Manor last night. I was—"

Jessica jumped up from the couch. "What were you doing at Pembroke Manor last night? And why were you snooping through Robert's stuff? I swear, Elizabeth, just because you don't like Robert is no reason—"

"Please, Jessica," Lucy interrupted, smoothly but forcefully. "I'd like to hear what Elizabeth has to say."

Jessica scowled at Elizabeth, but sat down quietly. When Lucy spoke in that commanding tone, it was hard not to obey. Besides, Lucy was one of the few people here whom Jessica had sincere respect for. Lucy wasn't afraid of anything.

"We all know that the newspaper has been covering up details of the recent murders, and that there are some similarities between the deaths," Elizabeth began. "Luke and I had narrowed down the possible murder suspects to three people: Lord Pembroke, Lady Pembroke, and the younger Robert Pembroke—"

Jessica opened her mouth to protest, but closed it when Lucy raised a warning hand.

"So I went to Pembroke Manor yesterday to find evidence that would implicate one of them," Elizabeth continued.

"I thought you were writing about ostriches!" Jessica interrupted.

"The ostriches were a ruse," Elizabeth admitted. "I only used them as an excuse to get out of town."

Lucy looked perplexed. "What is this about ostriches?"

Tony waved his hand. "Never mind that part right now. It's not important."

"Have you found any other evidence of young Robert's guilt?" Lucy asked.

Jessica tried to speak again, but Elizabeth cut her off.

"Yes," she said. "And I know Lord Pembroke has evidence of it, as well. I overheard a conversation between Pembroke and Andrew Thatcher. Thatcher knows Pembroke is protecting somebody. Apparently, Thatcher let him get away with it up until now, but Thatcher said the latest murder was the last straw. He gave Pembroke until ten o'clock tonight to tell him who the murderer is, or he'll subpoena him."

"So you never actually heard Robert's father say that Robert is a murderer!" Jessica said triumphantly.

"Actually, I did. Well, sort of. After Thatcher left, Robert's father said that the evidence he's found clearly implicates Robert, but that he doesn't believe it. He decided to call Robert and tell him to get out of town."

Jessica felt the color drain from her face. That explained Robert's sudden flight from London, and his evasiveness at breakfast that morning.

"That doesn't mean anything!" Jessica cried. "It doesn't prove that Robert is a murderer—much less a werewolf!"

Lucy raised her eyebrows. "A werewolf? You kids think the murderer is a werewolf? What kind of a cockamamie story is that?"

"It's true," Luke said quietly, his blue eyes blazing. "And it's not just us who think so. Even Pembroke and Thatcher believe it, if what Elizabeth heard this morning is any indication."

Elizabeth shrugged. "I know it sounds crazy, but look at the evidence. The victims' throats were ripped out, 'as if by a wild beast.' You said it yourself, Lucy. And I found fur on the door frame of the room where Joy was killed."

"The fur could have come from a number of animals," Tony pointed out.

"And even if it is from a werewolf, you can't prove it's Robert!" Jessica added.

"Well, I don't believe in werewolves," Lucy said thoughtfully. "But as journalists, we do have to consider every possibility. If this alleged werewolf is Robert, and he was wearing the green bathrobe on the night of Joy's murder, then we would, *theoretically*, find traces of fur on the robe. Fur that matches what you found in the door."

"Forensic studies should be able to tell us if the fur does come from a wolf," Tony said. "If we can find a police investigator who will examine the evidence for us, without tipping off Thatcher."

"I don't know about that, Tony," Lucy said. "Perhaps our best course of action now is to go to Thatcher with what we know."

"It's your call, Lucy," Tony said. "But Thatcher must have a lot of loyalty to Pembroke to have gone along with him this long. How do we know he won't bring anything we tell him straight to Pembroke Manor?"

Lucy frowned. "I suppose you're right. But that will complicate our chances of obtaining a forensic study of the evidence."

"Bumpo!" Elizabeth said suddenly. Everyone turned to stare at her. "Sergeant Bumpo loves doing forensic studies. And he's been thrilled to have Jessica and me covering his stories—nobody else ever acted as if they were important. He'll do it if we ask him to."

Tony nodded. "Good. I doubt a forensic study will prove that the murderer is a werewolf, but it could turn up other clues that could prove young Robert's guilt." He glanced at Jessica. "Or innocence," he added quickly. "I am glad to see that we're getting more out of your intern assignments than stories about exploding vegetables and murderous kitchen sinks."

Lucy raised her eyebrows again. "Murderous *what*?"

"Never mind," Tony said. "It's not important."

"Did Pembroke cite any other evidence for believing that the murderer is a werewolf?" Lucy asked.

"Nothing he said out loud," Elizabeth admitted. "But he and Thatcher both seemed convinced on that point."

Lucy crossed her arms in front of her and began pacing the living room. "As I said, I'm skeptical about this werewolf business. But I knew all along that Lord Pembroke was trying to hide something. I just didn't know what it was. Now, thanks to you, Elizabeth, it's clear. The evidence does seem to point to the conclusion that Robert Pembroke, the younger, is a murderer."

"No way!" Jessica protested. "I know him better than any of you do. Robert could never kill anybody—and he's not a werewolf!"

"But how else can you explain the threads from

his bathrobe, found at the scene of Joy's murder?" Elizabeth asked.

"What's so sinister about that?" Jessica asked. "It's his house, after all! Maybe he was in that room the day before."

Elizabeth shook her head. "I'm sorry if it upsets you, Jess, but you have to face the truth. Robert may be guilty of murder."

"Your life is in danger, Jessica," Luke warned her. "If you hadn't switched beds with Joy, you would have been murdered last weekend at Pembroke Manor. And you said yourself that someone attacked you in the tube station today."

Lucy turned to her, surprised. "Somebody attacked you?"

Jessica described the incident on the subway platform. Then she scowled at Elizabeth. "But it wasn't Robert!" she concluded. "Robert wouldn't hurt me—he loves me! I bet not one of you has come up with a motive for why he would kill me or those other people."

Tony and Lucy exchanged embarrassed glances.

"I'm afraid you've got us there," Lucy admitted. "Except that the murders clearly indicate a psychotic mind at work. Perhaps he doesn't even know he's doing it. I don't know, Jessica. I'm not a psychologist. But the evidence against Robert seems solid enough to warrant an arrest. And perhaps further investigations will reveal a motive."

Jessica shook her head. "No, they won't. Because he didn't have one. He didn't kill those other people, and he didn't try to murder me today. Besides,

Robert and I were supposed to spend today together, alone in the country. If he wanted to kill me, that would have been the perfect chance. But he didn't. In fact, he canceled our date at the last minute."

"Only because he had to leave town before Thatcher arrested him," Luke pointed out.

"No, no, *no!*" Jessica cried, her voice rising. "Wouldn't you leave town if you heard someone was about to arrest you for murders you didn't commit?"

Elizabeth laid a hand on her sister's shoulder. "But, Jess, who else but Robert could have been there in the tube station today? Everybody else thought you were out with him. Robert was the only person who knew you'd be alone. You've got to be careful, Jessica. You're in a lot of danger."

That was what Robert had said, Jessica remembered suddenly: *Promise me you'll be careful.*

"You're wrong about Robert," Jessica insisted. "I can't believe that he's any threat to me. But maybe you're right about the rest. Maybe I really am in danger."

With a shudder, she remembered the empty tube platform, the sound of heavy panting, and the brush of coarse hair against her bare arm.

"That's quite a painting!" David said on Wednesday afternoon, at the church of Notre Dame de France, on Leicester Square. The interior of the chapel was a little dim, so Eliana pulled off the sunglasses she'd become accustomed to wearing almost everywhere. Then she looked up at the cartoonlike mural, and smiled warmly when she felt David take her hand.

"It's a Cocteau, isn't it?" Eliana asked. "I've always been impressed with the way he combined surrealism with whimsy."

David looked at her with a mixture of admiration and curiosity. "How did you become such an expert, Lina? I wasn't aware that you knew about art."

Eliana smiled nonchalantly. "Oh, I've picked up a bit. I'm a voracious reader, you know."

She chastised herself for not being more careful. Expertise in art history didn't fit in with the image she'd built for herself. Why couldn't she keep her mouth shut? David already suspected that she was hiding something from him. All week, she'd been evasive whenever he'd mentioned Liverpool. And she kept slipping up—making remarks that were natural from a princess, but inappropriate from a working-class girl of sixteen.

Eliana sighed. The closer she felt to David, the more upsetting it was becoming to continue her charade.

"That's it," she decided under her breath, still pretending to be engrossed in the mural. "Portia has chosen tonight to tell her father the truth about herself. That's when I'll tell David the truth about me."

"Did you say something?" David asked.

Eliana blushed. "Oh, um, I was just noticing Judas up there on the mural—what an odd depiction!"

David laughed. "It certainly is. He looks a bit like the creature from the Black Lagoon!"

As they left the church a few minutes later, still

hand in hand, they passed an unusually crowded newsstand.

"Must be the evening edition of the *London Journal*," David said, dropping her hand to move close enough to buy a paper. "People seem frightfully excited over it."

Eliana held her breath as an inexplicable feeling of dread overwhelmed her.

"Look at the size of this headline!" David said a minute later. "Is this a newspaper or a billboard? Listen to this: 'Is Princess Eliana Dead?' Honestly, you would think that—"

Then he held up the newspaper and shook it open. Eliana saw with a sinking heart that an enormous photograph of Princess Eliana gazed serenely from its front page.

David's eyes widened and he did a double take. He turned slowly to look at Eliana. Then he examined the photograph again. Luckily, nobody else in the crowd was paying any attention to the two teenagers.

Eliana was afraid she was about to burst into tears. She wished fervently that she'd remembered to put her sunglasses back on when they left the church. She was sure that David recognized her.

I can't believe this is happening!

"David, I—" Eliana stammered. But she couldn't bear the look of shock and disappointment on his face. She had lied to him. And the real Lina—Princess Eliana, the daughter of the queen—was somebody a boy like David could never fall in love with.

Eliana shook her head helplessly, unable to meet his eyes. Then she spun on her heel and fled.

Lucy Friday wasn't the easiest person to get along with, Elizabeth decided. She could be brusque and overbearing, and was quick to judge people. But from the way Tony was smiling at Lucy, Elizabeth knew he loved her despite her aggressiveness—or maybe because of it.

"I have to admit, Lucy," he said as he held open the door to the *Journal* office. "It's great to have you back at the office, even if it is only for a visit."

Elizabeth, Jessica, and Luke passed by Tony through the open door, but Lucy stood outside with her arms folded. Elizabeth suppressed a chuckle. Lucy wanted it to be perfectly clear that she could get along without Tony's help—for opening a door, or for anything else. She had been certain that Tony was involved in the cover-up of the murder stories, in order to get the job of crime editor for himself. Now, at least, she seemed to realize that he was as perplexed by the cover-up as she was.

Jessica nudged Elizabeth's arm, and Elizabeth realized her sister had been thinking along the same lines.

"If nothing else," Jessica whispered, "at least this crummy murder mystery has brought Lucy and Tony back together again!"

Elizabeth smiled and nodded, somehow sure that things would work out this time between the two editors. But even more important was Lucy's role in the murder investigation. With an experienced journalist like Lucy helping, Elizabeth was sure they would have a solid case against Robert Pembroke in no time.

Elizabeth's hopes on both counts were quickly dashed.

When the little group filed into Tony's office, Lucy pounced immediately on the brand-new edition of the *Journal*, waiting on Tony's desk.

Lucy's beautiful brown eyes filled with suspicion as she read the lead headline. "That's seventy-two-point type!" she said incredulously, scanning the first few paragraphs of the article. "This is total rubbish. It says the body found at Pembroke Manor yesterday morning was the princess."

"I can't believe Reeves printed that!" Tony yelled. "He knew it was an unsubstantiated rumor. He was supposed to hold the story until I checked out the details at Pembroke Manor. What was he thinking of?"

Lucy spun toward him, furious. "Don't play innocent with me, Tony Frank! That's your byline, not Reeves's. You knew bloody well that this story was running in tonight's edition. Don't try to blame Reeves!"

Elizabeth shifted uncomfortably from one foot to the other. "Actually, he didn't know," she said, trying to help. "Mr. Reeves had Tony write up the story, but wasn't supposed to run it until—"

Lucy silenced her with a glance. "Save your breath, Elizabeth. I'm sick and tired of hearing people make excuses for this two-faced yellow journalist. You know, Tony, I used to think you had integrity, but the last couple weeks have shown me that *you're* the

163

scandalmonger, not Reeves. You're more interested in selling newspapers than you are in printing the truth. And then you have the unmitigated gall to pretend you're on the side of journalistic integrity."

"But Lucy, that's not—" Tony began.

"Well, I've had it with you!" she lashed out. "And I've had it with this newspaper. Don't ever call me again!"

Lucy stalked out the door, slamming it behind her with a crash that rumbled through the office like an earthquake. When the reverberation died away, the room seemed utterly still and empty without her.

"Well, I guess that's that," Tony said in a thin, quiet voice. "She's gone."

Chapter 12

Portia stood in the wings a half hour before the curtain was due to go up on Wednesday night's performance of *A Common Man*. Around her, crew members arranged lights and fumbled with pieces of scenery, while the cast hurried about in various stages of dress.

Portia, already in costume, stood apart from the others. She pounced on Jessica as soon as the American girl returned to the backstage area.

"Did you see my parents out there?" she asked. "Did they come?"

"I saw them all right," Jessica said. "They're out in the lobby where all the ticket holders are milling around waiting for the play to start."

Portia sighed thankfully. "I was frightfully worried that they wouldn't show."

"I could've found your folks even without the photo you showed me," Jessica said. "Jeepers, Mrs.

165

Bates wasn't kidding when she said your father was famous! Everybody in the place was hounding him for his autograph. All I had to do was follow the crowd!"

"Thanks again for coming along to provide moral support tonight," Portia said. Then she smiled conspiratorially. "Not to mention spying services."

"No problem! I love the theater, especially from this side of the stage. Besides, I was desperate to get away from my overprotective sister. Elizabeth has become a real pain in the neck."

"But doesn't she have some cause to worry?" Portia asked. "She told me someone attacked you in the subway today. Do you have any idea who it was? It didn't sound like a simple mugging."

Jessica shook her head. "I don't know who it was," she said. "But you're right—it wasn't a simple mugging." She sighed. "It's too long a story to go into now, Portia. Besides, I really don't want to think about it." She smiled mischievously. "And I'm surprised you haven't asked what I heard your father talking about in the lobby a few minutes ago."

Portia stiffened. "I didn't realize you were close enough to hear anything! What did he say, Jessica? He hasn't figured out that Penelope Abbott is really me, has he?"

"No, I'm sure he hasn't," Jessica said. Then she turned to watch as a tall, well-muscled young actor strutted by, wearing only the bottom half of his costume.

Portia gritted her teeth with impatience. "Jessica! What did my father say?" she screeched.

Jessica grinned. "Sorry. I heard your father say

he's heard a lot about this Penelope Abbott. He was glad to receive the tickets to come see her in action tonight. He has no idea who sent them, but that didn't seem to bother him."

"It wouldn't," Portia explained. "Theater people send him tickets to plays all the time. They're always anxious for his opinion on actors or directors or scripts."

"They're not the only ones who are anxious," Jessica said, taking in her nervous eyes and tense posture. "Relax, Portia, he'll love your performance."

"But what if he doesn't?" Portia asked.

"He will," Jessica said confidently. "What an exciting profession!" she exclaimed, looking as if she were drinking in the backstage atmosphere. "I always wanted to act. You know, I was Lady Macbeth in a production this year. And before that, I was in *Splendor in the Grass*. Everyone said I had a lot of talent. . . ."

Portia's thoughts wandered from the American girl's words. She was sure Jessica could be a terrific actress, if she ever settled down long enough to apply herself to one thing. But that didn't sound like Jessica. *Making a career out of acting takes constant work—constant attention. You have to devote your whole life to the craft.*

But that was all Portia had ever wanted.

Except for her father's blessing. When she first left home, Portia had convinced herself that she didn't need his permission to follow her dream. But she knew now that she would never be completely happy as an actress, unless she had his approval.

"I just hope he likes my performance tonight,"

she whispered desperately, interrupting Jessica's cheerful chatter. "He just has to!"

Elizabeth finished her narration of the day's events Wednesday night and sat down on her bed, watching to see Eliana's reaction.

"Your evidence sounds quite convincing," Eliana said, a startled look on her face, "especially the conversation you overheard between Lord Pembroke and the chief of police. But Robert Pembroke—a serial killer?"

"Even his father admits that the evidence points to him," Elizabeth said. "Of course, he's in denial about it. He doesn't want to believe that his son has committed such horrible acts."

She shuddered, remembering the blood-soaked sheets on Joy Singleton's bed.

"We'll have more details in the morning," Elizabeth continued. "I stopped by Scotland Yard this evening and dropped off the animal fur, the silk threads, and the green bathrobe with Sergeant Bumpo. He's happy to have an excuse to use his high-tech analysis lab. He'll call me tomorrow with the results."

"And have you figured out who the Annabelle person is?" Eliana asked.

"No. But she obviously loved Pembroke, a long time ago. Pembroke said she knew about the secret room—years ago. I was going to talk to Luke about her today, to see if he could speculate on her identity, but I forgot to mention it to him."

"I don't know how I could have been so wrong

about Robert," Eliana said. "He and I have never been friends, exactly, but I have known him all my life. He's always seemed a bit wild—but never dangerous!"

"The worst part about it is that I can't convince my sister that Robert's trying to kill her. She refuses to believe that he's really a werewolf."

"Actually, Liz, I'm with Jessica on that point," Eliana said. "Nothing you say can make me believe in werewolves, although I know that Lord Pembroke has been quite fascinated by them for many years. Apparently he's even persuaded Thatcher that the murderer is a werewolf."

"After what happened in the tube station today," Elizabeth said, "even Jessica is willing to admit that werewolves exist. But she's still sure that Robert is innocent. Eliana, I'm worried about her. Robert has killed four people! Jessica is in terrible danger until he's safely in custody."

"Where is Jessica tonight?" Eliana asked.

Elizabeth sighed. "She went to the theater with Portia. I suppose she'll be all right, in a public place like that. I made her promise she wouldn't go anywhere alone. Still, I wish she were here tonight, safe and sound in her upper bunk. Speaking of going out, Eliana, why are you sitting around here with *me* tonight? I thought you were spending this evening with David."

Eliana shook her head and tried, unsuccessfully, to blink back her tears. "Not anymore," she said. "And probably never again—now that he knows the truth about me."

Elizabeth gasped. "Oh, Eliana, I'm sorry! I didn't

know you were going to tell him this afternoon."

"I wasn't," Eliana said. "I didn't. I had decided to tell him tonight. But then that newspaper of yours came out with my photograph plastered across its front page. David picked it up as I was standing right there next to him, and . . ."

"And he couldn't help but notice the resemblance," Elizabeth finished for her. "I'm sorry, Eliana. I was hoping he would take the news better than that. What did he say when he realized you're a princess?"

"I don't know. I didn't tarry long enough to hear his reaction." She bit her lip. "Ah, Liz, I feel so foolish. Running away was fun for a while, but it didn't accomplish anything except bring grief to my family and David. And provide an excuse for Lord Pembroke to push the spate of mysterious deaths off of page one of the *Journal*."

"You can't blame yourself for Pembroke's actions," Elizabeth assured her. "And if David really loves you, your family's royal status shouldn't matter to him."

Eliana shook her head. "Even if the fact that I'm a princess doesn't make any difference to David," she said, "the fact that I hid it from him will. As much as I love him, it's over. David will probably never speak to me again. I just wish there was some way I could make it up to him."

"Maybe there is," Elizabeth said thoughtfully. "You can't go on hiding forever. Sooner or later, you're going to have to come forward—"

"It has to be sooner," Eliana realized with a sigh. "If I come out of hiding now, at least something good can come out of all this. We can prove that Pembroke was trying to cover up the stories about the murder, and get people to focus their attention on the real news story in London—the fact that four people have died horribly."

Eliana jumped off the bed and stood in the center of the room for a moment before coming to a decision. "Liz, I'm going to turn myself in."

Elizabeth grinned. "No, you aren't," she said. "*David* is going to turn you in."

"I don't understand," Eliana began. Then her eyes widened. "Oh, yes, I do understand! If David is the one to turn me in, then *he'll* get the million pounds of prize money that the newspaper has put up. With that he can endow the clinic he wants to start at the homeless shelter—and send himself to medical school so he can work in it! Elizabeth, you're a genius! After what I've done to him, I don't expect that David will ever love me again. But this way, I'll feel as if I've done something to compensate for the ghastly way I've treated him."

Suddenly, the door burst open, and David himself walked in. He stopped, flustered, when he realized Eliana was standing in the center of the room as if she'd been expecting him.

Elizabeth realized David hadn't seen her at all, as she sat on the lower bunk bed in the corner of the room. She opened her mouth to announce her presence, but David began speaking before she had the chance.

"Lina, or should I say Eliana," he stammered, beginning a speech that had obviously been rehearsed. "I loved you as a pauper. I'll love you just as much as a princess—if you'll have me."

Eliana's smile lit the room, and Elizabeth thought she looked as radiant as a princess should. "I will, David," she answered, smiling shyly, "under one condition."

Jessica stood backstage, listening to the echoes of the biggest standing ovation she'd ever heard—and imagining that she, rather than Portia, was the object of everyone's admiration.

But Portia certainly deserved the applause. Her performance as Isabelle Huntington that night had been remarkable.

After the curtain came down, Portia tackled her with a bear hug. "I'm so excited, Jessica! The entire cast was absolutely perfect tonight." Then her face fell. "But he's not back here, Jessica. The other cast members' families have made it backstage, but I don't see my father anywhere. He would come to see me if he liked my performance. He must have hated it!"

"Whoa, Portia!" Jessica said. "I've never seen you so keyed up. Give him a chance. The final curtain just came down. At this very moment, he's probably shoving his way through hordes of autograph seekers to get to you."

A pretty, waiflike actress tapped Portia on the shoulder. Jessica recognized her as Adrian Rani, who'd had a small part in the play. "Did you hear the news, Penelope? You'll never guess who was in the audience tonight—Sir Montford Albert, the Shakespearean actor!"

Portia managed a weak smile. "Oh, really?"

"He's been my absolute favorite actor for years!"

Adrian confided. Suddenly, her mouth dropped open and she pointed across the room. "Oh, Penelope, he's here! Montford Albert has come backstage! I'm going closer to see if someone will introduce me to him."

She scurried off, leaving Jessica and Portia staring across the cluttered space to the tall, distinguished actor who was scanning the room.

Suddenly, he saw the person he was searching for. When his eyes locked with Portia's, Jessica felt as if an electric current passed between the two. The other actors must have noticed it, too; the room fell silent. As he moved across the floor, the cast parted before him like the Red Sea.

Then, Sir Montford Albert wrapped Portia in a huge bear hug, while the other actors looked on, astonished.

Jessica was the only one close enough to hear his whispered apology

"I am so proud of you, darling," he said. "Can you ever forgive me for the beastly way I've treated you?"

Portia nodded eagerly, tears sparkling in her eyes.

"Way to go, Penelope!" yelled an enthusiastic young cast member.

At the mention of Portia's alias, Sir Albert looked up, realization dawning in his eyes.

"I think I understand what you've done, Portia," he said in a low voice. "And I know why you did it. But it won't be necessary anymore."

When he turned to the crowd, Sir Montford Albert was beaming. "Ladies and gentlemen," he announced grandly. "I'd like to introduce Portia Albert—my daughter, the actress!"

※　　　※　　　※

Lord Robert Pembroke was pacing again. It was eight steps across the gleaming parquet floor of his study at Pembroke Green, and eight steps back.

He had been fighting a wave of panic all day—ever since his telephone conversation with Robert that morning, when he urged his son to flee. He'd been unable to sit still since then—unable to eat or work or even to read his own newspaper. He'd made the trip into London, and locked himself in this infernal room, where he had reviewed the evidence over and over again, trying to find a flaw in the story it told. Now he was pacing.

He hated this room. In fact, he hated the entire house. Pembroke Green was his wife's domain; city living had never appealed to Lord Pembroke. He much preferred the open countryside. On his ancestral land at Pembroke Manor, he had a feeling of stability—of his place in time's continuum.

But now that continuum was about to come to a screeching, skidding, sickening halt, right at the foot of his heir and only son, Robert.

He consulted his watch for the third time in the last two minutes. His stomach lurched. It was exactly ten o'clock.

Somewhere in the distance, the doorbell rang. The sound was muted, but Pembroke's anxiety and the room's stillness magnified it into a harsh jangling. He pulled out a linen handkerchief and mopped the sweat that was running in rivulets down his face.

"Confound you, Andrew!" he said when Thatcher walked into the room a minute later. "Right on time, aren't you? You're like a vulture, diving in for the kill."

"An interesting choice of analogy, Robert," said the chief of police. "You have information for me, I presume?"

Pembroke stared at him wildly. "I'll tell you what the evidence reveals—though I still don't believe it, myself. But you must promise me that you won't release it to the media just yet."

Thatcher pounded his fist on the desk. "I'm not making any promises this time until I see the evidence, investigate it, and question the suspect. Don't you understand, Robert? Four people have been murdered! If I had followed my conscience after Joy's murder—" He stopped, shaking his head sadly.

"If I hadn't listened to you then," the police chief continued in a soft voice, not looking at Pembroke, "Maria Finch might still be alive today. No matter what the evidence says, Robert, her blood is also on my hands—and yours."

Thatcher turned to the older man, and Pembroke saw that his handsome face was hard, his mouth set in a grim line.

"Now, Robert, are you going to tell me what you know?"

The two men stared at each other for a full minute, but it seemed like an hour to Pembroke. Finally, he lowered his eyes, defeated. Then he reached for the top drawer of his desk, where he'd lovingly placed a handful of green threads, a clump of fur, and a silver cigarette case.

Chapter 13

Jessica practically stumbled over a scruffy-looking homeless man sitting on the sidewalk outside the *Journal* building Thursday morning, his face covered by a floppy old hat.

As she entered the newsroom, Jessica nearly stumbled again—this time over a row of rickety folding chairs that were stacked against the wall. In fact, she realized, the entire room was in chaos. A massive desk appeared out of nowhere and bumped toward her rapidly—carried, she saw, by two men in coveralls. Jessica scrunched against the wall to keep from being mowed down.

"What's going on here?" she called after them.

"We were told to move the desks out of the way to set up seats for a press conference, miss," one of the workers said in a cockney accent.

"A press conference about what?"

The man shook his head. "I sure as blazes don't

know, miss. I just move furniture."

The workers moved on. Jessica bit her lip, suddenly afraid. The only really big scoop she knew of was that the police would be looking for Robert soon. Could that be the topic of the press conference? Was her innocent boyfriend's name about to dragged through the mud?

She considered the possibility for a moment but rejected it. The *Journal* wouldn't hold a press conference on a murder investigation; the police department would do it. At least, she hoped so.

Then Jessica caught sight of Luke as he ducked under a huge boom microphone that a woman was setting up outside the door of Tony's office. She scrambled over to him. "What's the press conference for?"

Luke smiled sheepishly. "Sorry, Jessica, but your sister and Tony have sworn me to secrecy."

"Elizabeth knows about all this?" Jessica asked, gesturing around at the confusion. "I wondered why she was already gone when I woke up. But come on, Luke. Liz couldn't have meant *me* when she asked you not to tell anybody. Liz and I are identical twins. Telling me something is just like telling her!"

"Valiant attempt, Jessica, but Elizabeth specifically warned me not to say anything to you. I believe she mentioned something about 'a mouth the size of Westminster Abbey.'"

Jessica scowled. "Thanks a lot. Well, I see her near the copying machine, talking to Tony. Maybe I can wheedle it out of them."

She began striding across the room to confront

her sister. Then she remembered what Luke had said, and opted for a more subtle approach. She slipped behind a pair of desks that were stacked one behind the other and trained a practiced ear on her sister's conversation with the editor.

"Thanks for calling me last night with the big news," Tony said, "and for helping me arrange this press conference on such short notice."

Elizabeth smiled. "And thank *you* for letting me write a really big story—finally."

"It was an excellent article," Tony said. Then he smiled mischievously. "I suppose you've already prepared your acceptance speech for your first Pulitzer."

Elizabeth blushed, and Jessica knew she'd been dreaming of exactly that.

"What about the people back in the press room?" Elizabeth asked. "Certainly, they'll see the story when they print the newspaper. Can you trust them to keep it under wraps?"

"They're all sworn to secrecy," Tony replied. "In fact, they're printing the special edition right now. It'll be off the presses in time for the ten A.M. conference."

Jessica wished she had taken the time to flirt with some of the guys in the press room; maybe they would have told her the big secret.

"Will our special guests be here in time?" Tony asked.

"No problem there," Liz says. "What about Pembroke?"

"He'll be here, and I asked him to bring Thatcher, as well. I told Pembroke the gist of today's announcement, but not the details. I assume he's too distracted with his own problems to be angry at me for taking the liberty of setting all this up. If he's upset, I could be joining Lucy on the dole. That reminds me—did you call her? Is she coming?"

"It was a hard sell, Tony, but I think so. She's still angry with you, but I appealed to her journalist's sense of curiosity."

Tony rushed off to supervise the placement of the chairs, and Jessica leapt out from behind the desks.

"What was that all about?" she demanded. "What press conference? What article?"

Elizabeth gave her a smug, infuriating smile. "You'll know soon enough."

Elizabeth chuckled to herself as she saw Jessica's infuriated expression. Jessica had never been a patient person. Now she would just have to wait for the press conference to start, like everyone else.

Reporters from other newspapers were beginning to arrive. All they had been told was that Lord Pembroke had a major announcement to make. Now they were milling around the room, asking questions of one another and speculating about the answers. Elizabeth noticed Lucy, standing alone, and realized she was carefully avoiding Tony, though she had been too curious to stay away.

"Oh, well," Elizabeth thought. "At least she's here."

Jessica pointed toward the door. "Television cameras!" she exclaimed. "Does my hair look all right?"

"It looks fine, Jessica, as usual. But it won't matter. The BBC television people are not here to take pictures of you."

"You never know," Jessica said. "But look, there's Emily with the crew. *Some* media groups let their student interns come along on the big stories."

Emily caught sight of the twins and hurried over to them, dodging a radio crew on the way. Luke joined them a moment later.

"What's the big scoop?" Emily asked excitedly. "Do you *Journal* insiders have any inside information?"

Jessica scowled. "You know how much of an insider I am. If it doesn't deal with exploding vegetables, clog robbers, or falling kitchen sinks, I'm left in the dark. Elizabeth and Luke are in on the secret. Elizabeth even wrote the big exclusive in the special edition of the newspaper that's coming out today. But she's taken a vow of silence."

"Some of the BBC reporters think it's about the princess," Emily said. "Have they found her?"

Elizabeth shrugged, but kept her mouth shut.

"No way," Jessica said, with a speculative glance at her sister. "Liz couldn't have kept something that big from me."

"Here's Lord Pembroke now!" Emily said.

Lord Pembroke walked hurriedly into the room, followed by Andrew Thatcher. The men were obviously together, but there was a coldness between them that aroused Elizabeth's curiosity. And Thatcher's eyes looked blazing mad.

Luke took her arm and drew her aside from the others. "Do you suppose Pembroke told Thatcher about Robert at ten o'clock last night, as scheduled?" he whispered.

Elizabeth cast another glance across the room at

the two men. "My guess is yes. But Thatcher looks mad. I bet he's figured out that Pembroke told Robert to leave town."

"We've got every journalist in town assembled here," Luke pointed out. "I wonder if Thatcher will take advantage of the opportunity to announce a warrant for Little Lord Pembroke's arrest."

Elizabeth bit her lip. "I hope not, for Jessica's sake. I was counting on today's revelation to help people see that the *Journal* has been hiding the murders. But I'd rather see Robert brought in quietly."

"Any word from Bumpo on the forensic studies?"

"Not yet."

Elizabeth felt a tap on her shoulder. "Didn't anyone ever tell you it's impolite to whisper?" Jessica demanded. "Besides, something's happening over there." She pointed. "Isn't that yesterday evening's paper Pembroke is reading? He looks mad!"

Lord Pembroke folded the newspaper in a quick, jerking movement. Then he glared around the room. "Find Reeves!" he yelled to a terrified reporter. "I want him in my office, now!"

Then he stalked across the floor, ignoring the questions of a half-dozen journalists, and disappeared into his corner office.

A buzz of speculation arose from the gathered reporters. A moment later, Reeves emerged from his own office and strolled over to Pembroke's, a jaunty swing in his walk.

Elizabeth looked at Jessica, and both twins nodded. Then they motioned for Luke and Emily to follow as they slipped behind a row of stacked desks and picked their way, unseen, to a spot near Pembroke's door.

Lucy Friday obviously had the same idea. She was already standing near the door when Elizabeth led the others around the stacked desks. Lucy put a finger to her lips as the teenagers approached.

Reeves's proud voice filtered through the door. "Lord Pembroke, sir, I knew you would be pleased with this week's circulation figures. Yesterday's edition sold more papers than anything since the royal wedding. The princess death story really did the trick! Tony Frank didn't want to print it without more research. But I wasn't about to let him dictate editorial policy. The man's a neophyte—has no business sense at all! I went right ahead against his objections."

Lucy gasped, her face filled with shame and hope.

Pembroke cleared his throat. "I'll see that you get exactly what you deserve," he said in a voice so low that Elizabeth had to strain her ears to catch his words.

Reeves didn't seem to notice the forbidding tone in Pembroke's voice. "And today's special edition, sir, should top even yesterday's sales! I know you haven't seen the article yet, but believe me—it will be the scoop of the century!"

"And as I understand it, Tony Frank and his staff were responsible for the news we will reveal today."

"Er, yes sir," Reeves said, sounding confused. "But only under my direction, of course."

"Of course."

"Actually, sir, I would recommend replacing Mr.

Frank immediately. The man obviously can't handle his new responsibilities."

Pembroke's response was calm, but held a note of rage. "It is *you* who will be replaced," he said. "For knowingly printing an unsubstantiated rumor, your employment is hereby terminated."

"But, sir," Reeves stammered, "it was you who told me to play up the princess story instead of focusing on the murders, to find new angles—"

"What murders?" Emily mouthed to Jessica. Jessica shook her head, listening. These Americans, Emily thought, certainly had a taste for the morbid.

"I never told you to print lies!" Pembroke said, his voice rising. "Choosing to print one story over another is a simple matter of editorial judgment. But choosing to print a story that is not true is blatantly irresponsible. There is no room in my newspaper for lies! See that your belongings are out of the building by the end of the day."

The newsroom was electric with excitement as everyone prepared for the press conference to begin. Emily could feel it pulsing around her, in the hurried movements of the reporters and in their eager conversations. She fidgeted in her front-row seat between Jessica and Luke, and then turned to see if all the seats behind them were full.

"It's standing room only," she remarked.

"How about a hint, Liz?" Jessica pleaded, craning her neck to see her sister, who was seated past Luke. "Just give me a teensy-weensy little hint of what this is all about."

Elizabeth refused, and Jessica slumped in her seat, her arms folded across her chest. Emily knew she hated feeling left out.

"Cheer up, Jessica," she said. "There's a lot you can tell me. Who's the good-looking young man in front of the room, the one who seems so nervous?"

Jessica yawned. "Oh, that's just Tony Frank, my boss. Officially this may be Pembroke's press conference, but from what I gather, Tony's running the show. He's kind of a wimp, but he's a nice enough guy."

"Your friend Lucy can't seem to keep her eyes off him."

Jessica smiled. "You're right. I hadn't noticed. We've been trying to get those two back together all week. I'm glad it's finally working."

"What was Mr. Reeves saying earlier about covering up some murders? Nobody else even seemed surprised. I know a young woman was killed at Pembroke Manor last week. Have there been other murders as well? Does Lord Pembroke know who committed them?"

Jessica gasped. "No!" she said, loud enough so that several heads turned. "He doesn't know anything about who killed those people," she whispered. "The evidence is wrong!"

Emily was perplexed, but didn't want to provoke Jessica further.

Then Tony stepped up to the microphone, and the room quieted instantly.

"We've all been regaled for the last week or two with information and speculation about the disappearance of the queen's youngest daughter, Princess Eliana—"

A murmur rose from the crowd of reporters. Behind her, Emily recognized the frantic scratching of pens on notepaper and the furious clicking of keys on laptop computers. Had the missing princess been found?

"Lord Pembroke has an important presentation to make in a few minutes, but first I'd like to introduce somebody."

"That's Tony's office door he's pointing to," Jessica whispered. "Do you think he's got the princess in there?"

Emily held her breath as the door opened. Then she let it out, surprised and disappointed. David Bartholomew stepped out of the office, grinning nervously.

"What in the world is David the Bookworm doing here?" Jessica whispered as David and Tony conferred in low voices for a moment.

Emily shook her head, mystified. "I can't imagine a shy fellow like him speaking to all these reporters," she whispered back. Elizabeth and Luke, she noticed, didn't seem the least bit surprised.

Tony grasped the microphone again. "This young man is Mr. David Bartholomew, and he has a very important announcement to make."

David's voice was shaky when he began speaking. "I met somebody a couple weeks ago who seemed quite extraordinary. But I didn't realize just how extraordinary until yesterday evening, when I saw her photograph on the front page of the *London Journal*.

Ladies and gentlemen, allow me to present the Princess Eliana."

Tony unfurled a newspaper that Emily realized was a copy of the *Journal*'s hot-off-the-presses special edition. A huge headline blazed across the top of the page: "Eliana Is Found: University Student Turns in Missing Princess."

Then Eliana herself stepped out of Tony's office, looking quite regal in a white silk dress, with her hair piled on top of her head. But her hair was brown, instead of blond. . . .

Emily nearly fell off her seat. *The princess was Lina Smith!*

Jessica, next to Emily, was opening and closing her mouth like a guppy. Only Elizabeth sat calmly, not the least bit surprised.

"We've been living with a real, honest-to-goodness princess," Jessica blurted out, "and we didn't even know it!"

Tony's assistant passed out copies of the special edition as Lina (*Eliana*, Emily reminded herself) held a whispered conversation with Tony, David, and Lord Pembroke, who had joined them at the front of the room.

"Congratulations, Liz!" Emily said, impressed with Elizabeth's first page-one byline in the *Journal*. Elizabeth was beaming. Then Tony's assistant leaned in to whisper something to her. She jumped up and walked quickly to the corner of the room, where Emily saw her taking a phone call.

"What was so frightfully urgent that she couldn't wait until after the press conference?"

Emily whispered to Jessica, who shrugged.

"Thank you all for your concern in the last few weeks," Eliana said into the microphone.

"As you can see, the rumors of my death have been greatly exaggerated," she continued. The reporters laughed, but Emily thought that Lord Pembroke looked uncomfortable. "I have not been to Japan. And I most assuredly did not elope with a member of the palace guard."

"What happened to the Liverpudlian accent?" Emily whispered to Jessica.

"She's so poised and polished," Jessica marveled, "like . . . a princess!"

"In reality," the princess continued, "I behaved a bit badly, and I apologize for any grief I may have caused my family and anyone else." She smiled at David. "I ran away from the palace because I felt the need to escape the royal lifestyle. I wanted to learn what life is like in the real London. And thanks to a few special new friends, I have learned a lot—a lot more than I ever dreamed, actually.

"I spoke with my mother, the queen, last night, and I have agreed to return to my family today. But there will be some changes. I will no longer be cloistered in the palace; I will be free to associate with whomever I please." She glanced warmly at David. "But the most important change is that I will begin using my position to help people."

Emily heard a murmur of skepticism from the reporters behind her. The princess apparently heard it, too. Eliana thought for a moment. Then she removed the microphone from its stand and moved closer to the crowd, speaking more casually.

"On my way here today, I saw a homeless man, only half a block from this building. He was crouched on the sidewalk, his clothing old and torn. A large hat obscured his face, as if he were ashamed to be seen. That man, and others like him, represent the real London. A few weeks ago, I barely knew of the existence of that London. But since then, I've been disguised as a Liverpudlian named Lina." She smiled and fingered her brown-dyed hair.

"Lina obtained a position, working in a London soup kitchen. In that soup kitchen, Lina has seen sights that Eliana would never have been exposed to. Lina has met hungry, sick people—many of them children—with no place to live and few places to turn. Now that I know about that London, I want to use my position to change it. I plan to work for the poor, providing publicity and fund-raising efforts to homeless shelters, soup kitchens, and similar facilities throughout the city."

This time, the murmurs Emily heard behind her were of admiration.

"As you all know, Lord Pembroke, the owner of the *London Journal* and a distant relation of mine, has generously offered the sum of one million pounds for my return. In a few minutes he will present a check for that amount to David Bartholomew. Before he does, I'd like to tell you what David plans to do with that money, because I'm sure he's too modest to tell you himself."

David blushed bright red.

"David plans to donate that money to a London

189

homeless shelter, to go toward a clinic where the poor can receive free medical treatment. The royal family will make up the rest from my personal trust fund, and has agreed to put David through medical school—on the condition that he agree to head up that clinic as chief physician, after his graduation."

As the audience applauded wildly, Emily sighed, watching Eliana and David gaze into each other's eyes. "Don't you just love happy endings?" she whispered to Jessica.

Jessica sighed, too, but she sounded wistful. Emily remembered that Robert had disappeared the day before.

"Any word from Robert?" Emily asked her, as the reporters began questioning Eliana and David.

Jessica shook her head and blinked rapidly, as if she was trying not to cry.

"I'm sorry," Emily said. "I guess you must miss him a lot."

"I do," Jessica whispered back. "I love Robert, and he loves me!" She cast a venomous glare at Elizabeth, who had just returned to her seat. "I just wish some people would mind their own business, and stop spreading terrible stories about him."

Elizabeth had a stricken look in her eyes. "I'm so sorry to have to tell you this, Jessica," she whispered, motioning Luke and Lucy to gather closer, as well. "That was Sergeant Bumpo on the phone, with the results of the forensic study."

"Bumpo?" Emily asked, amused. "Isn't he the funny little chap who handles Scotland Yard's lost dog cases?"

For some reason, the others looked terribly serious. Dead serious.

"The silk threads definitely came from Robert's robe," Elizabeth said. "And the analysis also showed traces of fur on the robe—the same fur that was found in the doorway."

Jessica's face lost all color. "Somebody planted it there," she whispered. "I know they did."

"That's not all," Elizabeth continued. She took a deep breath and turned to Luke. "Bumpo hasn't completed the analysis of the fur, but he's certain of one thing—*it definitely came from a wolf!*"

"I don't understand any of this," Emily said. "What's going on?"

Luke shook his head at her. "It's a long story," he said. "And this is no place for a lengthy explanation."

"I'd better fill Tony in on the results," Lucy said quickly, rising from her seat. From the warm light in her eyes, Emily guessed that discussing the evidence wasn't the only thing Lucy had on her mind.

Suddenly, a reporter from another newspaper jumped to her feet and pointed with her pencil at Andrew Thatcher, who had been standing off to one side.

"Chief Thatcher," she asked loudly, "you have been searching for the missing princess for two weeks, with no luck. Why is it that the entire London police department could not find one missing girl—while two teenage tourists were able to break the story?"

Thatcher stalked to the microphone, annoyed.

"Hasn't the media wasted enough time on this story?" he asked, staring at the reporters in disgust. "With all due respect to the princess and the royal family, there is a situation afoot in London that is exceedingly more momentous."

The room quieted. At Emily's side, Jessica was absolutely still, her face still ashen.

"My department has a suspect in the murder of Joy Singleton," Thatcher announced. "And that suspect is also wanted for questioning concerning the deaths of Dr. Cameron Neville, Nurse Dolores Handley, and Maria Finch, a cook at Pembroke Manor. The victims all bled to death, from wounds on their throats—rather like the mauling of a large animal. The police will make the arrest"—he cast a dark glare at Lord Pembroke—"as soon as the suspect can be located."

"Murder?" Emily whispered to Jessica. "The newspaper said the doctor died of natural causes! And what's this about a cook. . . ."

She stopped when she saw that the American girl wasn't paying any attention to her. Instead, Jessica was staring at Thatcher, shaking her head as if she were pleading with him. Remarkably, Lord Pembroke had adopted exactly the same posture. Emily had no idea what was happening.

Thatcher stared grimly at Pembroke and shook his own head almost imperceptibly. Then Pembroke sighed and walked, with a heavy tread, out of the building.

After watching him leave, Thatcher took a deep breath and made his final announcement, in a voice that revealed a mixture of determination and regret, but mostly just exhaustion.

"A warrant has been filed for the arrest of Sir Robert Pembroke, Jr."

Jessica felt as if she were plunging into a deep, black pit. The chief of the London police department was standing in front of her, calmly telling a group of reporters that the boy she loved was a psychotic killer. At least he hadn't mentioned the werewolf theory.

"Lord Pembroke is cooperating with the police in every way," Thatcher said in response to a reporter's question, "though he firmly believes that his son is innocent."

Jessica caught a sarcastic glance between Elizabeth and Luke.

"If he thinks his son is innocent, then why did he skedaddle out of here?" another reporter demanded.

"Lord Pembroke is understandably distraught. But he has assured me that he does not know his son's whereabouts at the present time."

Elizabeth reached over to lay a hand on Jessica's arm. Suddenly, Jessica's despair turned to fury.

"This is all your fault!" she hissed, knowing her voice was covered by the chaos that had followed Thatcher's announcement. Some reporters were rushing to the phones to call their offices, others were shouting questions at Thatcher, and a third group had torn out of the room, in pursuit of Pembroke.

Jessica focused her rage on her sister. "That's what you were being so secretive about last night. You must have called Thatcher with your so-called evidence against Robert—even after we agreed nobody would go to the police with it!"

Elizabeth shook her head. "No, Jessica. I didn't call the police. I was being secretive about the princess story. It was Tony I called last night, to set up this press conference. I didn't know Thatcher would make this announcement."

"Yes, you did, because you told him to!"

"Calm down, Jessica," Elizabeth urged. "It must have been Lord Pembroke himself who told the police about the evidence. Remember Thatcher's ultimatum—he wanted the truth by ten o'clock last night."

Jessica jumped from her seat. "It's not the truth!" she cried. "And Lord Pembroke never would have turned over evidence about his son. But you would! You've hated Robert all along!"

"Yes, that is correct," she heard Thatcher saying calmly. "We have established a connection between a total of four deaths, and we now believe them all to be murders—violent, grisly murders."

Suddenly, Jessica saw the body of Dr. Neville, sprawled on the floor in a pool of blood that stained the floral carpeting. She saw Joy's blond head, looking so much like her own, in the midst of crimson-spattered sheets. And she felt coarse hair scrape against her arm, while the sound of heavy panting echoed through the deserted subway station.

Robert was not the murderer—or a werewolf. But somebody in London was. And until he was found, Jessica knew that her own life was in danger. Suddenly she felt more vulnerable than she had ever felt in her life. Without Robert here to protect her, she would have to rely on herself. Somebody bumped one of the bright television lights, and its reflection caught Jessica's eye, flashing off the anti-werewolf pendant that hung around Elizabeth's neck. A shiver skated down her spine, but Jessica thought about Robert's strong arms and warm kisses, and she swallowed her fear.

"I love Robert," Jessica said aloud, though nobody was listening to her. She straightened her shoulders and looked around her with a new, grim resolve. "And I'll do whatever is necessary to clear his name."

Bantam Books in the Sweet Valley High series
Ask your bookseller for the books you have missed

SIGN UP FOR THE SWEET VALLEY HIGH® FAN CLUB!

Hey, girls! Get all the gossip on Sweet Valley High's® most popular teenagers when you join our fantastic Fan Club! As a member, you'll get all of this really cool stuff:

- Membership Card with your own personal Fan Club ID number
- A Sweet Valley High® Secret Treasure Box
- Sweet Valley High® Stationery
- Official Fan Club Pencil (for secret note writing!)
- Three Bookmarks
- A "Members Only" Door Hanger
- Two Skeins of J. & P. Coats® Embroidery Floss with flower barrette instruction leaflet
- Two editions of *The Oracle* newsletter
- Plus exclusive Sweet Valley High® product offers, special savings, contests, and much more!